DEVON'S PAIR

JAYNE RYLON

OTHER BOOKS BY JAYNE RYLON

DIVEMASTERS
Going Down
Going Deep
Going Hard

MEN IN BLUE
Night is Darkest
Razor's Edge
Mistress's Master
Spread Your Wings
Wounded Hearts
Bound For You

POWERTOOLS
Kate's Crew
Morgan's Surprise
Kayla's Gift
Devon's Pair
Nailed to the Wall
Hammer it Home

HOTRODS
King Cobra
Mustang Sally
Super Nova
Rebel on the Run
Swinger Style
Barracuda's Heart

Touch of Amber
Long Time Coming

Compass Brothers

Northern Exposure
Southern Comfort
Eastern Ambitions
Western Ties

Compass Girls

Winter's Thaw
Hope Springs
Summer Fling
Falling Softly

Play Doctor

Dream Machine
Healing Touch

Standalones

4-Ever Theirs
Nice & Naughty
Where There's Smoke
Report For Booty

Racing For Love

Driven
Shifting Gears

Red Light

Through My Window
Star

Can't Buy Love
Free For All

DEDICATION

To all fans of the Powertools Series. Your continued support has blown me away. Because of you, I can assure you this won't be the final chapter in the crew's story.

Thank you!

PROLOGUE

Neil swiped work-scuffed knuckles over his gaping lips to ensure no drool escaped. He couldn't help but stare. Painted toes peeped from strappy sandals. They led his bulging eyes to a delicate ankle then up the pretty, tanned calf that poked beneath the open door of a beastly black truck. The sexy shoe rested on the running board before its equally delicious owner hopped down to street-level right outside the crew's current fixer-upper.

Maybe the pick-up wasn't any bigger than the one he and James owned. It could have been the sultry yet petite driver who made it seem as enormous as the whale sharks he and his boyfriend had spotted while snorkeling in Mexico last year. There too, most anything would have seemed gargantuan beside the glorious plum smuggler that had hugged James's svelte hips as though he'd been shrink-wrapped into it.

Neil shook his head to clear the tropical memories of his lover. Between them and the chance run-in with this woman—one he'd love to lure inside and share with James—he'd be sure to sport wood when he met their new employee.

The lecture James had delivered on their ride in this morning resounded in his mind. *"Try to tone it down until we get to know him, okay? The new guy might not be as accepting as the rest of the crew of our wild liaisons."*

Not many people were.

Wouldn't be good if their recently hired apprentice quit before lunch.

The dude hadn't showed yet, which meant Neil had to hang out here on the curb and wait for the schmuck. A mutual friend had highly recommended Devon Giles right when they'd decided they could use some temporary help. Most of the rest of the crew settled into new relationships and needed a little extra personal time compared to usual. After a bunch of debates, they'd agreed to try adding someone to their tight-knit group on a trial basis.

Running late on day one wouldn't earn the guy any brownie points.

Still, the sweet view made up for abandoning James, who'd already started tearing up the shitty old flooring by himself. Neil hated to let his partner shoulder more than his fair share. Generous and hardworking, his mate would push himself harder than he should. Neil swore he'd make it up to James with a killer back rub and slow, relaxed sex.

Maybe sooner rather than later if he ate his fill of such sweet eye candy.

The woman sauntered around to the other side of her truck and caused Neil to wonder if he was dreaming when she shucked her cornflower blue peasant blouse right there in the soft light of the spring morning. She left her racer-backed sports bra in place as she kicked off those sinful shoes and covered her cute pink pedicure with thick white socks before slipping her dainty feet into sturdy...construction boots?

What the—?

The petite-yet-toned woman's jacked arms flexed as she strapped a canvas tool belt around her miniscule waist. A hammer hung from one of the loops over her khaki cargo shorts. She flipped a pair of sunglasses onto her head. The eyewear, which had more in common with safety goggles than designer shades, pinned her cute bob of ash blonde hair off her striking face. The swell of her perfect ass stunned him as she reached into the truck. Next thing he knew, she had retrieved a large water bottle, locked up the vehicle and headed in his direction.

It was then he met her gaze. An uncommon shade of gorgeous jade-green eyes, which he'd only seen once before—on James—snared his attention. Her seamless mix of tomboy charm with pixie sass entranced him. When she noticed him and smiled, offering a small wave as she approached, he realized he was royally screwed.

The world popped into slow motion. His heart stuttered in its pounding beat and the ground lurched below his feet as he experienced the same supposedly once-in-a-lifetime sensation he'd had the day he'd met James, when their professor assigned partners in their trade school lab.

Love at first sight.

Oh, fuck.

***

Devon cringed when the hottie construction worker's smile morphed into a major grimace.

Not again. Damn it.

Her sister's roommate had rambled on and on about the *amazing* crew when she'd spotted the opening for an apprentice in an online job ad. Julie had promised Devon the all-guy team of five was forward-thinking, accepting and had a lot to teach her, though she refused to go into detail on how she'd learned of their reputation.

Give them a chance, Dev.

"Good morning. I'm…"

"Devon Giles. Of course." He scrubbed his hand through his messy hair before taking her fingers with a measured action more suitable for reaching for a viper than a trainee. "I was expecting someone—"

"With a dick?" She canted her head and planted her fist on her hip, daring him to deny it while hoping she'd misinterpreted his sour puss.

He barked out a laugh. "Well, yeah, I suppose."

"Look, if this is going to be an issue, I'd rather head out now than waste time—yours or mine. I'm a damned good worker and—"

"Hey." A man with a soft, kind voice interrupted her rant before the gorgeous, but assholish, guy could backpedal. "I thought I heard someone pull up."

Did she imagine the way the new arrival brushed against the first guy as though he were a cat winding around his owner's ankle?

"Ah…"

The taller guy grunted. "Yeah. *This* is Devon."

"Pleased to meet you." The smaller man's shake was firm, which she appreciated. She didn't need them to make any concessions for her. "I'm James."

"And I'm Neil." The original guy surprised her by pressing a kiss to her knuckles.

"Okay, Romeo." She had to nip this shit in the bud or it would spiral out of control. After the last job she'd had to leave—when the foreman deluded himself into believing she'd take orders to bend over as well as she did instructions on leveling framing jobs—

she wouldn't risk giving anyone the wrong idea. "Enough of that nonsense. Would you have done that if I were the man you expected this morning?"

"Maybe. If he were as cute as you are." He laughed when James smacked him on the ass.

Holy shit. No mistaking the easy, familiar contact or the heat in the men's eyes when their gazes met and locked. Maybe she *had* found the perfect employers. If they were gay, they might leave her to work and develop her skills in peace.

The spring was looking brighter by the second.

CHAPTER ONE

"Dev, could you grab another tube of caulk off the back of my truck? This one isn't going to make it." Dave had squished his mammoth frame into the standard tub to run a bead around the base of the tile work she'd installed with his guidance. Of course, she'd added a little of her own flair to the design. As she surveyed it now, she had to say it'd come out better than she'd imagined.

Rewarding her for a job he approved of, Dave had done the grunt work and saved her back some strain. Pleasing the crew could be tough. The guys had lofty standards. In the past three weeks, she'd learned tons and had started surpassing their expectations. When she did, they made sure she knew it.

Dooming Dave to unfolding and refolding that stunning body would be torture. For both him and her, watching. "Devon?"

"Sorry." She cleared her throat. "Yeah, I've got it. Be right back."

She jogged down the hall. Plastic sheeting covered new hardwood planks that made her light footfalls crunch in the long, empty space. Mike and Joe perked up as she trotted past the master bedroom where they were installing recessed lighting, which would add some flair to the space.

"Hey, Dev. You two almost ready for lunch? I'm starving." Mike looked pretty damn hungry when he glanced in her direction. Silly to wonder if that smoky look meant anything more than desire for the packed meal his adorable fiancée had shipped him off with this morning.

"Mmm. Yeah." Joe rubbed his flat belly. Dear God, did they have to work without shirts so much? It was enough to drive any red-blooded woman insane. "Morgan's testing out new cookies again. She sent a big box for us to share."

"And how many did you eat for breakfast?" She loved teasing the crew.

"As many as I could shove in my mouth on the drive in." He winked at her.

"Well, we all know your mouth is capable of some pretty amazing feats." Mike poked Joe in the ribs with the handle of his needle-nose pliers. "Hand me that housing so we can wrap up. Tell Neil and James they've got about fifteen minutes 'til break."

"Right-o, foreman." She saluted then jumped when Dave's yell reached her loud and clear.

"Dev! You coming or what? I'm going to be pulling a Taft soon."

"Definitely or what," Joe bellowed for her, somehow still managing to pout. "We're not that lucky. Give her a second. Mike distracted her. Besides, if you get stuck I know where to find some lube."

"Don't you usually grease up to try and get in, not out?" Mike's wicked grin sent shivers along her spine.

She pretended to dismiss his dirty implications with an eye roll and a little finger wave then continued her jog down the stairs. Thank God they couldn't tell how slick the tops of her thighs were. They were guys. Five of them, in all their sweaty and sexy glory. Holy testosterone overload. They couldn't help themselves and somehow their equal opportunity jokes didn't bother

her. They aimed them at each other as often as they did at her. Being left out of the good-natured teasing probably would have made things awkward.

Luckily, she didn't know for sure. The crew had made her feel at home from the moment James had saved her from that uncomfortable start with Neil on the curb outside this house. The renovations had come a long way in the past three weeks. Within a month they'd be wrapping the place up with a big ass ribbon for the future owners. Moving on from the project she'd come to associate with her mentors would suck. Between the crew and their women, she'd instantly inherited eight new friends. Spending the spring with them would be no hardship.

It was leaving at the end of the internship that worried her. Maybe if she buckled down and absorbed as much as she could from them, they'd have a permanent spot for her as they headed into summer and the end of their three-month arrangement.

Lost in her thoughts, she didn't hear the rustle of denim on denim or the soft moans echoing in the vacant living room until it was too late. Devon burst onto the main level of the house, where Neil was making a late-morning snack out of James's parted lips.

She lurched to a dead stop.

Move. Look away. Keep going.

Devon couldn't force her legs to walk on past. Not when the fire between the two men burned hot enough to have tiny beads of sweat dotting her upper lip. She licked the salty sheen, wishing she could taste the partners' passion instead.

Pure devotion laced every tender sweep of James's fingers over Neil's bare shoulder, warring with the desperation of their mouths, as though they couldn't stand to be apart. Yet she could see the warm spring sunlight from the bay window behind them streaming between their torsos.

A golden beam cut through the dust in the air. It led her stare to the juncture of the men's bodies. They hadn't embraced closer because Neil fisted a double helping of beefy cock in his right hand, massaging their erections in time to the flicker of their tongues. He squeezed their shafts together. The tip of his cock tucked against James's balls though James's hard-on only reached most of the way back to Neil's groin. With a firm grip—much harder than Devon would have been comfortable administering—Neil made several circuits with his fist, drawing a sweet whimper from James.

The plea morphed into a groan as Neil's hand shuttled faster between them. James arched his hips, still wrapped in the ripped jeans he wore so well. The fly had been left open, allowing the V of denim to frame his cock. Devon wished she could see Neil's fine ass, but his pants remained mostly in place.

Would he guide the pair toward the inevitable conclusion of their escalating exchange? Or would he yank his hand free, bend James over the nearby sawhorse and ride...

"Devon!" Dave's holler broke through the steam fogging her brain.

She jumped several inches off the brand new hardwood planks, which the duo making out in the corner had laid this morning. Her boot knocked into a forgotten scrap board. It launched in the couple's direction, skittering across the unpolished surface with a scratchy racket they couldn't ignore.

James blinked.

He met her gaze, his eyes widening when he caught her spying on their break.

"Oh my God. I'm so sorry." Her cheeks blazed. She hadn't considered their privacy. Not that they should have expected any here. Still, she could have respected their relationship instead of ogling them as if they were stars in a seedy peep show.

Worse yet, when had her fingers strayed between her legs, pressing on the soaked crotch of her cut-off jean shorts? She stumbled backward.

"Dev, wait." Neil took a stride in her direction. His rock-solid cock bobbed and waved. He cursed as he tried to tuck it inside the unzipped flap of his jeans. As if that measly scrap of fabric had any chance of obscuring his impressive erection from view.

She bolted for Dave's truck, planted one palm on the open tailgate and boosted herself into the bed. In less than ten seconds, she'd snagged a tube of caulk at random and hustled up the driveway to the garage entrance. No way was she retracing her steps.

How could she face Neil and James after copping a self-feel at their display?

How could she have resisted the genuine love urging them to take the opportunity to bond? She'd never seen anything so beautiful in her whole life. Not even the gardens at Versailles that she'd studied endlessly in hopes of adding landscaping to her list of handywoman skills.

***

"What the hell took so long?" Dave grunted. "My knees are turning into ground beef. Now I get why Kay hates blowing me in the shower. I'm never suggesting it again. Unless... Hmm. I could always hold her upside down, use the wall to—"

"Gah!" A strangled gurgle escaped her throat. Were they *trying* to give her a heart attack?

"Shit. Sorry, Dev. I forget you're not one of the guys sometimes." He winked. "Planning to give me that caulk or do you really think it's going to keep you safe from my wicked ways?"

She forced her fingers to uncurl one by one from the tube she hadn't realized she'd aimed in his direction like a gloppy version of a vampire hunter's stake.

"Seriously. Are you okay?" He tilted his head, his eyes narrowing. "I didn't mean to make you uncomfortable. Smack us upside the head if we get too wild for you."

"I don't think they'd have appreciated that," she mumbled below her breath.

"What?" Dave accepted the cylinder then frowned. "Devon, this is clear silicone. We were using white to blend with the grout, remember? Is that what took so long? If you're not sure of something just ask. It's okay. You're here to learn."

"For Pete's sake." She slapped her hands on the outside of her thighs hard enough to sting both the skin there and her palms. "I know the fucking difference between clear and opaque caulk."

"Whoa." Dave climbed to his feet with hardly a wince as he focused on her, his voice softening. "What's happening here?"

She hated the tremble in her quads. Surrendering to the weakness, she let it drop her to the closed lid of the horrid shell-pink toilet they planned to replace after they finished the shower. Her head felt like a fifty-pound bowling ball in her hands.

The big man, who'd just escaped the torture of the bathtub, crouched beside her, ignoring the pop and crackle of his poor joints. He rubbed one broad hand over her back in big circles. "Calm down, sweetheart."

"Don't fucking call me that." She may have objected, but she couldn't make herself brush off his platonic touch. "Would you use frilly nicknames for the rest of the crew?"

"Yeah, he probably would." Mike leaned against the jamb, nodding to Dave when the other man shot him a clear *mayday* look. "Devon got an eyeful of Neil and James trying to sneak a quickie. We warned them about trying shit like that these days."

"Damn it." Dave rubbed his temples.

"Does *these days* mean since I've been around?" Could she be cramping everyone's style? What rabbit hole had she tumbled down if that were true? This time *she* might be the one causing discomfort on the job site by forcing team members to repress their sexuality for fear of making things awkward.

Ah, crap. How was that for karma?

There was a difference between asking assholes at prior sites to keep their hands off her ass every time she bent over and forcing two men obviously in love to hide their affection.

Okay, so maybe there'd been too much for anyone's official workplace standards going on in the living room. If she'd forced them to keep a lid on it for weeks, it was no wonder they'd erupted in a spectacular display of passion. The two of them had the real deal. She refused to allow jealousy to turn her appreciation green.

"I think we'd better have a staff meeting. Come on you two. We'll eat our lunches and talk this through with the whole crew." Mike addressed them both though his warm eyes melted on her. "No slouching, newbie. You didn't screw up. They owe *you* an apology."

"No—"

Mike waved her off before she could explain. "Save it. We'll figure things out together."

She stood and accepted a hand from both men. Though their broad shoulders wouldn't permit them to walk side by side, they didn't let go as they formed a chain and headed downstairs together.

CHAPTER TWO

Devon grabbed her reusable lavender lunch pouch from the pile on the kitchen counter. The pretty bag stuck out like a sore thumb in the mix of dented aluminum boxes and crumpled paper sacks. She couldn't help humming a snippet of that old Sesame Street song, "One Of These Things (Is Not Like The Others)".

Neil had claimed the red plastic cooler, which was far too large for one man's sustenance even considering the astounding stomach capacity the guys in the crew possessed.

What other enormous appetites could they have?

Refusing to give in to the urge to huddle in the corner and let Mike navigate the tricky waters they'd found themselves in, Devon inserted herself between Neil and Joe, who leaned one hip against the crappy Formica they hadn't yet replaced with granite. His long, powerful legs were stretched out and crossed at the ankle.

"Could I get a boost?" She smiled when he nearly encircled her waist with his long fingers then lifted her as though she weighed less than a bag of cement. Tucking her legs under her in the front, she sat cross-legged, pleased to be somewhere near eye level with most of the crew.

"Sure thing, pipsqueak." Joe ignored her glare in favor of scooping up his prime sandwich for another colossal bite that demolished a fourth of the generous entrée in one fell swoop.

"Is that fresh-baked wheat?" Her mouth watered. Suddenly her PB&J on Wonder bread with a side of baby carrots and celery sticks didn't sound so appealing.

"Yeah, want a taste?" Joe ripped off a piece of the bread and held it out. "I think Morgan added some honey and oats or something. She's a goddess."

Devon didn't think anything of eating it from his fingers until she caught the strangled groan from Neil. Her knee brushed his ribs, which fluttered against her in time to his rapid respiration. Maybe he and James hadn't finished their session after her extra-rude interruption.

"Devon—" he began as she also spoke.

"I'm sorry. Didn't mean to ruin your fun." When James attempted to cut her off, she only talked louder. "Believe me, I understand what it's like to hide in plain sight. I would never wish that on anyone else. I hope that you won't let having me around change your behavior. If the rest of these guys can handle watching you two *work* together, then so can I."

"As enticing as that offer is, I'm not sure you know what you're asking for, Dev." Neil angled his torso toward her, his hand coming to rest on her stacked ankles. She tried not to thrust her pelvis at him when his knuckles brushed her pussy. Mistake or not, she didn't care. A persistent throb had taken up a slow, steady pulse in her core. He had the ability to soothe it. If only he weren't already in a relationship with a man he adored.

"Uh, the unintentional demonstration you gave was a pretty good indicator." She bared her teeth, hoping she looked like she was smiling instead of flashing a big-bad-wolf grin. All the better to eat them with. They'd been delicious together.

"That was nothing." James slinked toward her, coming to rest along Neil's side. A mysterious twinkle in his eye roused her curiosity. She tuned in to his teasing smirk. Did James bait her...or his boyfriend?

"Oh really?" She refused to be cowed. "Then why were you about to crawl inside him?"

"I think what James means to say is that we're used to doing a hell of a lot more together than jacking off. What you witnessed was only the tip of the iceberg." Mike corralled the crew, ensuring they didn't veer off course when so much remained unspoken.

More than *that*. She blinked.

"Really? And who's *we*? I've met your girlfriend, Dave." She waved her hand at Joe and Mike. "And your fiancées. Are you trying to say you're cheating on them? With each other?"

"Hold up a minute with the stink eye. We'd never lie to our girls." Mike corrected her. "They know everything. They've all played along at some point or another. More than once if you want the truth. And, well...

We're still figuring things out. It's new. Different. We've sort of settled on an unofficial look-but-don't-touch policy. And we all reap the benefits of sharing those stories at home."

"Mmm." Joe's moan echoed three times louder than the one he'd surrendered at the taste of his lover's cookies. "Morgan *loves* hearing about what kind of trouble Neil and James get into. And when the four of us meet up, well, sometimes things evolve."

"Except *these days* I've been keeping you all apart?" She glanced from man to man.

Joe pushed potato chips around the paper plate he'd set his sandwich on. Dave studied the paint splatters on his jeans, and James reached for Neil's hand.

Mike swallowed hard then manned up. "Yeah. I'm sorry, Devon. We shouldn't have put you in the middle like this. We thought long and hard about bringing someone else into the crew. You're really a great addition. I'd swear we've known you a lot longer than a few weeks. You work hard, you learn fast and you never complain. You're fun to work with, and you've earned our respect. I think that's why these two felt comfortable enough to revert to our old tricks."

"Plus Neil is sporting a boner every time you're nearby." Dave winked at her. "That's got to make it hard to get work done."

"What?" she sputtered. She'd thought the pair was gay. Were they saying she worked with five sexy and sweet bisexual men? *Wow.*

Joe slapped Dave upside the head. "When will you learn to think before opening that big mouth?"

"You never complained about my mouth before." Dave parted his lips and wiggled his tongue in his friend's direction.

"Holy shit." She clutched her pounding heart and rocked herself like a trauma victim.

A hush descended over the usually boisterous men. She'd never heard them so quiet or seen them so still. It was almost as though someone had sculpted five perfect figures and replaced the guys with decoys.

"Does it bother you that much to think of us screwing around with each other?" James tipped his head.

"What?" The blood rushed from her face. "You think I'm grossed out?"

"Look at you." He reached toward her slowly, laying a gentle hand on her shoulder.

He massaged her tense muscles with a steady, mild pressure.

"You're right. I'm upset." She bit her lip, trying to figure out how to explain.

Dave muttered a curse in the background.

"But not by the thought of you…sharing…each other and your girlfriends." Did they notice her fidgeting as she tried to contain the desire bubbling within her like an effervescent spring?

"Then what's wrong?" Neil laid his shaking fingers on her knee.

Devon swore a current flowed from his hand to James's, which lingered on the other side of her body. Electricity arced between the two points, lighting up every nerve ending between them. She shivered. "I thought I'd grown close to you all. Like a part of the team. And all along I've forced you to obscure who you really are. What you really feel. I've become everything I hated about the crews I worked with before. I've done to you exactly what they did to me—making me erase any traces of femininity so that I didn't upset their delicate sensibilities. I stole your freedom."

"To be fair, we didn't give you an option." Mike scrubbed his face. "I think this is my fault, not yours. I convinced the guys it'd be better this way. I should have known we can't change our nature. We've been spoiled. Indulged our cravings for close to a decade. Quitting cold turkey was never going to work."

Was he referring to her joining the team or to the changes they'd made after hooking up with Kate, Morgan and Kayla? She couldn't help them with the bigger picture, but she could solve her piece of the puzzle.

She plucked her unopened lunch bag from the counter. Her appetite might never return after she did what she should. Still, she scooted toward the edge of the counter. "I agree."

"You do?" Neil aimed a broad smile in her direction. The gorgeous expanse of his brilliant white teeth mesmerized her for a moment.

"Yes." She sighed. "So I'm sorry to say... I quit."

"What?" Dave whipped toward her so fast she flinched.

"Settle down." Mike put a restraining hand on his friend. "No one's going anywhere yet."

"I won't cramp your style." She shook her head.

"You're telling me you don't want to see the grand finale?" Mike crowded her, tucking in tight beside James, invading Joe's territory. The rest of the crew observed and she swore she didn't spot a single one of them blink. "Be honest, Devon. You liked what you saw. I can smell you. Hell, even upstairs I could tell."

She tried to cross her legs. No room to move. Suddenly there seemed to be hard bodies closing in from every side. Like a castaway floating in shark-infested waters, she suddenly imagined she could be dessert.

"I've known these guys a long time." Mike shifted his focus to Neil and James. He studied them for a while before continuing. "Unless I'm completely off the mark, there's potential here for something great. Something new. Dave might have been crude, but he wasn't wrong. Neil has it bad for you."

"What?" She whipped her head around to face the tall, lanky construction worker.

"Of all the crew, you've been the least friendly. I thought I finally knew why. I'd be grumpy too if I were sexually frustrated all day."

Like she'd been for the past three weeks.

"No, honey." James saved his partner from explaining. "I think he was trying to keep his hands to himself. I was teasing him about it earlier. The way he watches you. I kept telling him to imagine what it'd be like if he asked you to play. If you said yes. That's what pushed him over the edge, made him take the risk. I'd give this man anything to make him happy. And he does want you. Something fierce."

She considered James's unasked question. Could she trade an afternoon of pleasure for potentially ruining an amazing job? Wouldn't it all be over anyway if she couldn't find a way to go forward?

Devon took a deep breath then pretended to be a hell of a lot more bold than she felt. She turned toward Neil and peered deep into his eyes. She read desire there. In response, she unleashed the matched answer from her center. It had infuriated her to find him so damn attractive. Especially when she'd thought he wished she was the normal guy he'd expected that first day. Now that she knew the truth, she couldn't resist.

His hair was soft between her fingers as she took hold of the unruly waves and tugged him to her for a scorching kiss. Initiative dissolved under his delayed assault. He came to life, as though his boundaries melted at the first contact of their lips. After what seemed like an eternity, she tilted her head before she suffocated. He'd stolen her breath.

A groan reminded her of their audience. Especially this man's lover. She cleared her throat.

"What about you, James? Is this what *you* want?" Power filled her when she focused her vision only to discover the naked longing in his gaze. "To watch your boyfriend with a woman?"

"Works for me. Especially if I can have a taste of you too." He leaned closer to nibble a path down her arm. When he reached her hand, he took her middle finger into his mouth and sucked. The tip of his tongue flicked against her sensitive pad in a swirling figure eight that left her gasping.

"No kidding." Neil rumbled a laugh behind her. "He's fucking amazing. The things he does with that mouth should be a crime."

"Show me." She panted. "Show *us*."

CHAPTER THREE

"Hell yes." Joe abandoned the rest of his sandwich. He rushed into the other room and snagged a freshly laundered drop cloth. They'd planned to use it to protect the floor they'd just finished laying. The canvas rumpled as he shook it out over the open space where the breakfast nook would normally be.

A squeal escaped her when Neil growled and scooped her into his arms. She clung to him like a baby koala, wrapping her arms and legs around his fine body.

"That's right," he crooned. "I won't drop you."

His hands squeezed her ass before he tipped forward, depositing her on the makeshift bed Joe, Dave and Mike ringed. James knelt beside her, pillowing her head on his thigh.

Neil stared into her eyes and then those of his lover. "Gorgeous. Your eyes. They're exactly the same. A perfect match. My favorite color."

James wiggled his brows at Neil. "Now how about you admire hers up close and personal. Kiss her again. Make love to her. I want to watch you let go."

"Wait!" The five men froze instantly at Devon's protest. "I won't steal this from James. I saw how bad he needed you before."

"There will be plenty of time for that later." James stroked her cheek. "He's dying for you. It's been growing over the past few weeks. Give him what he needs. Please?"

"Thank you." Neil looked back and forth between her and James. "Thank you for understanding. Thank you for sharing."

Devon sighed when the men kissed above her. She stared at them. Their mouths clashed and soothed over and over. Her hand snaked to her mound again, unable to ignore the ache there.

"*Ahem.*" Mike cleared his throat in a rather exaggerated chuckle. "Don't forget our guest so soon."

"And what about you?" It unnerved her to see so many faces hovering above her as she wobbled on the edge of surrender.

"Will it bother you if we jack off while we watch?" Mike didn't hem and haw, he cut straight to the chase. "God, it's been so long."

She bit her lip and shook her head. Is this what it felt like to be the star of a play, with so many watching on the fringes of the action? For the first time, she understood how that rush could be addictive. She had her own show as they unfastened their pants.

Holy crap. "Is this really happening?"

"Only if you're okay with it. Tell us if it's too much." Neil sank low over her. The pressure of his erection tucking against her swollen mound through their clothes inspired a wave of delight to break over her. Still, he didn't devour her. The hard shell he'd maintained for weeks cracked, revealing something tender and gentle beneath. "They're right, you know."

"About?" Her concentration fractured with so many distractions. Soft groans fell on them like gentle rain from the showers that had fed the blossoming flowers lately. Mike, Dave and Joe rubbed their chests and hard abs. They dipped long fingers into their pants as Neil and James seduced her.

"How much I want you." He nibbled a path from her ear to her jaw. "From the first moment I saw you. I needed this. You."

"You didn't know me." She rolled her eyes. "Don't be ridiculous."

"There's something about you. You're tough, compact and still so damn adorable." He rubbed their noses together. "I'm sorry I didn't make you feel welcome. There was no way I could without doing *this.*"

His fingers inched up from her hip. They tucked beneath her black tank top with built-in bra. He caressed her ribs then fit his palm over her smallish breast. "A perfect handful."

"Here. Let us see what you're feeling." James reached between her and Neil. He snagged the hem of her shirt and walked it up her torso.

Devon helped by raising her arms, allowing him to peel off her top.

They worked as a team. Neil didn't bother to unbutton her cargo shorts when he shimmied them from her hips.

She wished she'd worn something flirty beneath, but she'd come to work, not frolic in the attention of her five spectacular bosses despite what they'd done in her dreams last night. Her lack of sexy lingerie didn't matter anyway. Neil dispatched her white bikini briefs with little ceremony. Completely bare, she held still as he stared at her, laid out before him.

"Jesus, she's pretty. You know how to pick 'em." James muttered, still supporting her shoulders so she lay at a slight incline.

"Damn straight." Neil grinned at his partner. "I claimed you, didn't I?"

The rest of the crew chuckled though the sound held an edge she didn't remember hearing in the past. Their corded necks and heavy breathing assured her she hadn't imagined it.

Neil ran his hands over her flat belly toward the soft, bare skin above her pussy. James took over where his boyfriend had left off, cupping the gentle swell of her breasts and brushing his thumbs over her beaded nipples. The dual approach had her struggling to keep her eyes open. No way was she about to miss out on the scrumptious scenery.

"No fair." She didn't worry that a whine carried her objection.

Neil's fingers brushed the top of her slit, dipping into the slickness coating her bare lips as her hips rose to meet him. He didn't seem very apologetic when he asked, "What's that, Dev?"

"I want to see you too. All of you." Whether she meant Neil naked or the entire crew bare, well, it didn't really matter. Both were honest desires.

Devon didn't have to ask twice. The distinctive *whoosh* of well-worn denim surrounded her as five men shucked their jeans. She would have liked to have the willpower to resist checking out their tools but who could deny themselves that kind of eye candy?

Her eyes widened as she realized just how much fun the men's lovers had gorged on. With bodies like those and the skill she knew they harnessed in using them... Well, it was a good thing only James and Neil were left unattached or her head would probably have exploded from passionate overload.

Dave chuckled. "Thanks. That look never gets old."

"I bet." She tried to ignore the spike of unwarranted possessiveness prickling her. Exactly how many women had they treated to the full-crew special? Why did it matter?

She'd amuse herself and run. No muss, no fuss.

"You're cute when you're jealous." Neil pinched the side of her ass.

"I am not—"

He crushed his mouth over hers, aligning their bodies. Skin on skin. She couldn't have protested even if she wanted to. Oh God, he was so hot. A thin sheen of perspiration broke out across her chest, helping him to glide over her as he captured her lips in a scorching kiss.

Sometime after, stars danced in her vision.

"Let her breathe." James tapped Neil on the shoulder. "You're squishing all the air out of her."

She inhaled deeply when Neil slithered down her body. Open-mouthed kisses didn't help her regulate her respiration. Neither did his tongue, licking a path over her abdomen. "I can't get enough of the taste of her."

"Eat her pussy." Joe's usually calm voice reverberated with a gravelly growl she'd never heard before. "Make her come. Take the edge off. She's as jumpy as you have been all month."

"Is that true?" He lifted his head. The vulnerability in his dilated pupils shot a nail through her heart as surely as if she'd misfired the pneumatic gun they used.

"Yeah." She smiled when tension evaporated, making him more handsome without the stress lines around his eyes and mouth. "I need you too. You've been killing me. All of you. Strutting around with no shirts on all the time. Hot as hell. I've never felt this way about guys I worked with before. I wondered if I was losing it."

James petted her with slow strokes through her hair. He cradled her head on his lap and traced her lips with the tip of one finger. "I should have talked to you sooner. I'm sorry I waited. I'm sorry I let you doubt yourself."

She didn't question her instincts. Instead, she angled her face until she could lap at his erection, which stood proud against his abdomen. His cock wasn't heavy enough to weigh itself down so she opened her mouth and sucked lightly on his balls instead. With the tip of her tongue, she flicked the base of his erection.

"That's right." Mike encouraged her when James seemed to lose his voice. "Neil isn't big into blow jobs. Go ahead and treat James. It's been a while since he's had good head."

Usually she didn't care to go down on guys. After all, it was sort of like shooting herself in the foot if she wanted to be well fucked. But with two studs at her service, why not?

Devon opened her mouth and peered up at James.

"Yes." He hissed as he tipped his stiff erection toward her lips and tucked it inside. "So hot. Damn."

She got so into sucking his shaft—a comfortable mouthful—that she yelped when Neil settled deeper between her thighs and treated her pussy to similar attention. Her spine arched off the floor, giving him a perfect place to grip her waist. He capitalized on the leverage to tuck her tight to his skilled mouth.

James cupped her jaw, tracing her lips where they encircled his shaft. "Slow down, sweetheart. Or I'm not going to last."

She attempted to smile with her mouth full, but didn't change her pattern.

"Shit."

"Five bucks says James comes first." Joe drew her attention as he bet Dave.

"You're on. Neil saves all his oral skills for pussy." The bigger man's hand seemed to speed up as it drew on his beefy erection. "Kay says he's the best. Devon's gonna tip over in record time."

She hated to cost him the wager, but she'd never been a speed orgasmer. Most guys couldn't take her there at all without a little help from her hand. Impossible to facilitate with James clenching her fingers in his fists. She smiled as she tore her stare from the three men stroking themselves to monitor her prey.

James clenched his jaw so hard she worried about his dental bills. For about half a second anyway, until Neil distracted her with insistent pressure from his suckling lips over her clit. He took his time, exploring a variety of motions, until he did something amazing with his tongue that had her squealing around James's cock.

The shock of intense pleasure kept her from surrendering in the first instant of his treatment.

"Shit, I think you might have made a good call," Joe grumbled to Dave and pumped his cock faster.

Mike grinned. He slid closer for a better view. "I'm studying up. Kate loves it when I steal your tricks."

Neil hummed, only making Joe's demise a little more likely. She retaliated, concentrating on drawing the salty pre-com from James's pulsing erection. Mike reached out a steadying hand when his friend tilted off balance.

"Oh. Jesus. Yeah." James's fingers clenched in her hair. "Feels so good, Devon. More. Just like that."

She obliged eagerly. Every flick of Neil's tongue inspired her to reach out to the man in her mouth. Every press of Neil's lips and graze of his teeth had her mimicking his actions. The swell of passion that ballooned in her, causing tension to tighten her empty, aching pussy, inflated to astronomical proportions.

Her thighs quivered. She held stock still, afraid to move for fear of shattering.

"Damn. Damn. Can't hang on." James could have read the thoughts straight from her mind.

Either the creamy taste of his first jet of come or the insertion of one of Neil's long fingers in her pussy pushed her over the edge. She couldn't say which for sure. Perfectly timed, they triggered her orgasm together.

Devon swallowed greedily. The flex of her throat worked in time with the spasms gripping her channel around Neil's embedded hand.

She wished it had been his cock instead.

James collapsed beside them, laying his head on her breast. She rubbed his back with one hand as he soothed her belly with one of his own. Neil rose above them with a fierce shout. "Condom. Now."

Mike must have dug one from his wallet. He held it out and ready.

Neil's hands shook as he rolled it over his cock. When he fumbled for the third time, Dave reached over and finished sheathing his friend.

"Thanks."

"Don't mention it." Dave licked the glaze of pre-come from his fingers before resuming his measured stroking over his stiff hard-on.

"Are you ready for me?" Neil sat on his heels between her thighs. "Or do you need some time to recover."

"Is he always this considerate?" Devon turned to James.

He kissed her gently then smiled. "I think he's afraid of breaking you. You're even littler than me. After fooling around with these hulks, you seem like a china doll."

"But you know better, right?" She could relate to James. It had to be hard being the smallest of the bunch. "Put him inside me. Don't make me wait."

"Yes, ma'am." James fisted Neil's sheathed erection and guided it to her slick entrance. "You heard her, Neil. She needs to be fucked. Don't think. Just do it."

Devon gasped when the blunt head of Neil's cock stretched her open. It'd been a while for her. The lingering spasms of her orgasm tensed the rings of muscle at her entrance.

"Let him in," Joe called out to her. "He's almost through. It'll get easier."

"Breathe, Dev," Mike added.

They didn't understand. It wasn't agony—no, it was ecstasy—that had her crying out. She opened her eyes and locked stares with James when Neil relented, backing off on the pressure driving his forward motion.

"No." James grabbed Neil's ass and forced him closer. "Keep going. Give her more. She needs more."

"Ah. Yes!" she screamed when Neil buried himself to the hilt.

He began to thrust inside her. Long, deep glides left no part of her untouched, unexplored. James lowered his head to take her nipple between his lips. He plied the hard tip with his tongue and sucked it against the roof of his mouth while his other hand roamed across her torso to make sure neither of her breasts were left out of the fun.

"So hot." Joe groaned from beside them.

Neil didn't respond. His focus stayed entirely on her. He pumped inside her again and again. Sweat trickled over his hard pecs and the defined ridges of his abs.

Why couldn't this last all day? This euphoric bliss caused by being the center of the crew's universe. At least temporarily.

Rhythmic grunts accompanied the shuttling of Neil's cock, loudest each time he bottomed out in her pussy. The three men surrounding the trio on the floor inched closer until their knees touched the entwined threesome.

James allowed his fingers to cruise down her center until they found her clit. He rubbed gently yet fast, in a maddening loop around her swollen nub. The combination of his fluttering touch and the pounding of Neil's pelvis had her curling her nails into her palms to keep from coming.

Not yet. Not yet.

"Let go, Dev," James whispered against her breast. "They're waiting for you to shatter. Look how badly they need to join you. Let go."

She forced her eyes to open. Each man around her met her gaze as she let them see everything they made her feel. When she returned to Neil, she had no choice. Her body betrayed her, clamping around his shaft, savoring the defined ridges of the veined tissue and the thick head of his cock.

Just as her spasms began to die down, a groan echoed in the empty kitchen. Warm fluid spurted onto her chest and belly in time to the jerks of Dave's cock. Joe and Mike joined in as though the sight of their friend's surrender tripped a switch inside them. They drizzled their pearly come onto her torso.

Neil yanked himself from the quivering tissue of her pussy and stripped his condom off in one motion. He aimed his cock at her and assisted his partners in decorating her tan skin. Several spots of his release dribbled onto her bare pussy. She swore the weight of the droplets caused another orgasm to roll through her.

As everyone soaked in their shared release, something warm and soft lapped against Devon's skin. She pried her heavy lids open to observe James cleaning every last bit of the mingled mess from her body. He hummed as he devoured the essence of his friends and lovers.

"That was the best staff meeting I've ever been to." She winked at Mike. "Impressive staffs for sure."

"I give you a ten for BJ skills. Seriously though, negative points for the jokes, Dev." Joe ruffled her hair.

She buried her face against Neil's chest and giggled. Thirty more seconds. Then she'd force herself to get dressed like the rest of the guys, whose clothes rustled somewhere farther away than the pounding of her heart, which gradually slowed.

"Thank you." Mike laid his hand on her knee and squeezed before climbing to his feet. Dave and Joe followed his lead, leaving the three of them to recover in relative privacy.

"You were amazing." James spoke when Neil seemed incapable of expressing himself. "You gave him everything he needed and more."

"And you?" She couldn't put her finger on when it had happened but she'd developed a connection to James. A bond she hadn't expected.

"The same. Thank you." He kissed her forehead then stood to pull on his jeans.

"Break's over." Mike hollered from upstairs. The laugh in his tone had them chuckling along. The man was hardcore, but not a hardass. More like he provided an out from the potentially awkward situation. "Get back to work, kids."

"On it, foreman." She smiled as she rolled to her feet and tugged on her clothes.

Neil surprised her by catching her shoulders before she scooted off to finish the bathroom with Dave. He tucked her close, laid a long, sensual kiss on her parted lips, then spun her in the direction of the stairs and smacked her ass.

What did it say about her that she loved it?

She peeked over her shoulder for once last glimpse of him. Instead, she caught James sparing her and Neil a longing glance. At least she thought so. But when she squinted, he only smiled from his spot a few feet away.

***

"Great job today, guys. And girl." Mike clapped Joe on the shoulder. "We're ahead of schedule so I don't see any problem with taking the weekend off."

"Good thing." Dave perked up. "You know how much Kay has been looking forward to the barbeque on Sunday. The resort is almost ready to open, and she's dying for you all to share it this one time before guests start arriving."

Devon had heard oodles about the clothing-optional facility Dave's naturist girlfriend had built from the ground up, with the crew's help.

"And..." He cleared his throat, drawing interested glances from the rest of the gathering. "I was sort of thinking about asking her to marry me. This weekend I mean. Maybe at our bonfire."

"You've had the ring forever." James beamed. "Do it already. She's not the kind of woman who requires something elaborate. Just the place you share. Make it official. Ask her."

"I will. When the time is right." Dave sighed. "Maybe when you're all there."

"I think it's best if we each take tomorrow to think about our future." Mike spoke carefully. He'd obviously given the topic some consideration this afternoon. They'd worked twice as efficiently as before. Devon hadn't realized how much she'd been screwing them up. "Come prepared to talk. All of us, together. We need to make some big decisions about where we go from here. Ignoring things aren't going to make them any better. I'm not willing to fuck up the most important relationships in our lives. Not with our wives. Or each other."

Every crew member nodded. Except Devon. Where did she fit in?

"You'll be joining us too." Mike didn't phrase it as a question.

"I—"

"Please." Neil turned to her and enfolded her hand in one of his. With the other he reached for James, but his partner had taken a step back at some point. "Say you'll come."

She sucked in a huge breath and held it as she considered the plea in his eyes. Next she considered the open invitation in each of the other guys' answering nods. When she locked her gaze on James, she wavered. He stared at the juncture of her and Neil's fingers, not into her eyes.

"I don't think..."

James lifted his head and scrunched his brows. "You have to come. Neil needs you."

"What about you?"

"Let's take that time to think first." Mike stepped forward, breaking her connection with Neil. "Nobody say anything they'll regret."

They shuffled toward the door then dispersed as they angled for their vehicles. She hopped into her truck. The door hadn't shut yet when Joe, parked beside her, called softly, "See you Sunday."

"I don't know where I'm going." If that wasn't the statement of the century she couldn't have said what was.

"I'll email you directions. And if you need, Morgan and I will pick you up. We won't let you get lost, okay?" He smiled.

"Promise?" She wished she could hug him.

"Yeah. I promise. And so do they." He lifted his shoulder. She followed the invisible line he drew to where James, Neil, Mike and Dave watched their exchange with eagle eyes.

"All right then. I'll see you on Sunday." She backed out of the driveway, surprised by the unshed tears blurring her vision.

When had they come to matter so much?

CHAPTER FOUR

Devon sat in the driveway, her truck parked behind the usual assortment of oversized construction vehicles. She tugged on the hem of her simple cotton dress, still wondering exactly what ensemble was appropriate for a clothing-optional facility. A solid hour and a half trying on everything in her modest closet—again and again—hadn't made her any more confident she would avoid a fashion faux pas.

At least Kate, Morgan and Kayla had seemed completely cool and relaxed the times she'd hung out with the whole group. They'd never make her feel out of place. Unless they disapproved of what had gone down at the job site on Friday.

A giant sigh ruffled the short bangs framing her face. She reached over and retrieved the simple veggie assortment she'd prepared as an offering. Not like she could whip up her mom's famous spice bread—her usual potluck contribution—when a professional baker would be in attendance.

Pitfalls loomed around every twist and turn in her relationship with the crew. What the hell had she gotten herself into? Maybe she should bolt before they spotted her.

"Need some help with that?" Mike's greeting hammered the last nail in the coffin of her fledgling escape plans.

Damn it.

"Nah, I got it. Thanks." She tried to smile. Her muscles were too tense.

He ignored her and nabbed the tray from her hands. Good thing or she would have dropped it when she realized he strutted around the property in the buff. Muscles gleamed and flexed in the late afternoon sun.

The smell of grilling burgers wasn't responsible for her sudden drooling affliction.

By the time she'd recovered even a tiny fraction of her wits, they'd reached the front porch. Kayla ran out to greet her with an enormous hug. Devon didn't flinch from the warm skin that met her hands when she returned the embrace. In fact, the toned expanse of Kayla's back felt soft and warm. Comforting. Something about Devon's reaction must have clued Kayla in to her confusion. She retreated and narrowed her eyes.

"Sorry," Devon chuckled. "Not quite sure how this works."

"You're our guest." Kayla's smile seemed natural and light as she took the platter from Mike and shooed him off with a wave. The women headed inside together. "Do, or don't do, whatever makes you comfortable. It's a clothing-optional resort, not a clothing-prohibited one. It took Kate and Morgan a little while to loosen up enough to join in. No one will think poorly of you if you're not ready."

"Hey, I heard that." A clatter from the kitchen announced the infamous cook was putting the finishing touches on their dinner. "Besides, I'm still not nude. I'm wearing an apron."

"Safety first." Kayla grinned as she turned toward the prep space in the open cabin.

Devon would have followed but the enormous floor to ceiling windows caught her attention. She wandered over for a better view of the gorgeous valley and the lake at the bottom. Instead of rustic charm, she caught sight of Neil and James chasing each other around the rear of the house.

Bare-ass naked.

Her breath rushed out.

"Like what you see?" Kayla asked.

"The view is amazing." Devon blushed as she realized how true her cover up statement turned out to be.

The other woman only chuckled. "Right you are. On both counts."

Kayla had a way of making Devon feel at home. What could have been awkward turned out to be organic. She was the only one making a big deal out of the bare skin deal.

When in Rome...do as the naturists do.

Devon gathered her skirt and pulled her light dress over her head. She glanced into the yard, the fabric dangling from her fingers, just in time to watch James smash into Neil. The taller man had stopped dead in his tracks. His gaze locked on her body, framed in the window. James shook his head like a dog emerging from the water then followed his partner's stare.

He laughed and tossed her a finger wave before smacking Neil on the ass, stealing the soccer ball she hadn't noticed before, and tearing off through the lush grass.

"Well, that's one way to make an entrance." Kate wandered from the kitchen with a dish in her hand. She looked even lovelier than she had in the little black dress she'd sported the last time they met up for dinner out. Somehow, she made naked seem like the new trend in designer eveningwear, complete with sedate pearl earrings. "So glad to see you again. I think the guys were worried you wouldn't come."

Devon didn't have the heart to admit they were right to be concerned.

"It's okay, hon. All of us were overwhelmed at first. Still are at times. It's a lot to get used to. No rush and no worries, okay? Want to bring your tray this way? I'll show you where we're setting everything out."

"Thanks." She swallowed past the lump in her throat. She should have known they'd make this easy for her. They were some of the coolest people she'd ever met. Reality was, it scared her to think of losing them so soon after becoming an honorary member of their bunch.

She'd spent her whole Saturday dreaming of what it could be like if her temporary position became something a hell of a lot more permanent.

"Dev!" Joe beamed at her from his place tending the grill. "Looking good."

Morgan swatted him half-heartedly with a hand towel as they arranged the last of the food. "Behave yourself."

He grinned then snagged his fiancée, dragging her close for a sweet kiss that had the potential to turn into something downright smoky. When they touched, so simply though completely, Devon understood the difference between a casual encounter and a soul-deep bond.

What they had was the real thing.

Kate coughed. Maybe the char wasn't all a product of the couple's searing kiss. "Hey now, Morgan. No distracting the chef. I don't like my burgers *that* well done."

"Fine, fine." Morgan removed her tongue from Joe's mouth and stuck it out at Kate. "I *am* getting pretty hungry."

"You know, I can round someone else up to do the honors here if you need me to feed you a little appetizer." Joe wiggled his brows. "Has that picnic table been christened yet, Kay?"

The tall, tattooed woman whistled a little ditty.

"Should have figured you two have nailed each other on every rock and up every tree on this mountain by now." He shook his head.

"Jealous?" Dave came around the corner with Mike, beers in hand. He tossed one to Joe then settled onto the stone wall they'd built a few weekends ago.

"Nah, but I do approve." With a grin, Joe began to plate the meat as James and Neil trotted up beside them. They panted, out of breath from their game.

James jogged until he was within arm's reach of Devon then slowed to a stop. "Hi."

She let her hands hang, awkward, at her sides since she had no pockets to stuff them in. "Hey."

"Oh, damn. We're not doing this weird first-time-we-see-you-after-having-sex thing are we?" Neil strode right up to her and wrapped her in a tight embrace. He planted a juicy kiss directly on her lips before retreating. "I'm no good at pretending. I missed you yesterday."

"No mistaking that." Kate dropped her gaze to his solid hard-on. "That thing stood up and waved hello from across the field."

The group cracked up as they selected brightly colored plates from a stack and dished out the food they'd made together. The last traces of Devon's reservations disappeared with dinner. Great conversations, a generous helping of ribbing and easy camaraderie made her forget all her concerns. She didn't realize she'd shifted in her seat, leaning against Neil with her legs in James's lap, until the rest of the crew piled their plates in the center of the table.

"Guys are on clean up duty since the girls cooked." Kate stood and stretched. She claimed a fresh pitcher of the sangria someone had mixed up.

"Hey, I grilled." Joe's pout earned him a kiss on the cheek from Morgan.

"Too bad. It's time for girl talk. Come play in a little while." She patted his chest then sauntered after Kate, plucking a pair of fresh glasses from the supplies.

"Who are we to argue?" Kayla entwined her fingers with Devon's and tugged. "Wait 'til you see what Dave designed back here."

Devon glanced over her shoulder, pleased to see James's and Neil's gazes locked on the sway of her hips. She blew them a kiss.

"Are you teasing them or are you serious?" Kayla slowed as they sauntered down the hillside. She kept hold of Devon's hand, using it to guide her along the soft, sandy path fringed with pretty river rocks and flower beds. Perfect for bare feet.

"Uh…" Putting her heart on the line didn't seem wise. Especially when she hadn't gotten to talk to the two men, whom she'd dreamed of every second since Friday afternoon, about what had happened. She shivered a little. The setting sun made her wonder if she should run back to grab her dress. Though late in the spring, the nights still got chilly.

"Don't worry, you'll be warm soon. Unless you're screwing around with our friends. Then you might find yourself getting the cold shoulder. Neil has feelings for you. It's obvious to Dave, and after seeing you together tonight, I agree with his assessment of the situation."

"What?" Devon faltered on the path. Good thing the padded walkway absorbed her stutter steps.

"He treats you different than us. He's protective, like he is with James. He cares for me, Kate and Morgan. Hell, he's even fucked us silly from time to time. But with you... He's softer. Careful. I know things are happening fast, but I'm asking you to respect him." Kayla squeezed Devon's fingers again and led her into the glade ahead.

"I will." Devon cleared her throat then spoke louder. "I do."

"Good." Kayla smiled. "Then let's get nice and comfy. They've been dying to try this doohickey out. I want tonight to be perfect for all of us."

"What thing?"

"You'll see." They followed a curve around thick foliage. On the other side, Kate and Morgan were lighting several gas fire pits placed artfully around a patio. Crew-made waterfalls edged the rockwork. They fed a tangle of streams that meandered through the space. Tiny bridges crossed the wandering flows, which emptied into an asymmetrical koi pond near the center.

An enormous woven rope lounger stretched above the gurgling water. Plenty big enough to hold a dozen people comfortably, the modified web impressed Devon with its scale and creative use of the materials. For naturists, the air swirling around their relaxing bodies would feel like heaven.

She visualized lying face down, peering at the fish swimming in lazy circles below. Unlike a hammock, the netting was bolted at the four corners, preventing it from swaying too much.

"We can try out the new pads I sewed this week." Kayla opened the top of a cedar storage bin off to the side and withdrew puffy strips that would prevent the rope from digging into sensitive skin. A pile of blankets and pillows overflowed the rest of the large trunk.

Kate snagged one of each and climbed onto the mesh. She reclined, crossing her legs at the ankles as she stared up at the gorgeous colors streaking the sky. "You're going to make oodles on this place, Kay. I'm sort of sad we won't have it to ourselves much longer."

Morgan heaped Devon's arms full of pillows then she grabbed some blankets. They acclimated themselves to the surprisingly comfortable seating, taking advantage of the pads while each of them downed a glass or two of sangria. Chatter came easy—about their guys, the books they'd been reading, deals they'd scored at the mall the day before and life in general. They collapsed onto the bedding to study the emerging stars like pampered members of an elaborate harem.

"It's still a little nippy out for this." Morgan chaffed her arms.

"We can head inside if you want." Kayla tried not to sound disappointed. She failed miserably.

"No way." Kate scooted her pad closer to them. "Let's snuggle up. The guys will be here soon to keep us warm."

Devon didn't hesitate when Kayla patted the spot beside her. Warmth from the fire pits paired with heat waves rolling off her new friends to keep her nice and toasty. She relaxed, not caring that her head rested on Kayla's shoulder. Stress and worry over what might or might not come to pass seeped away. Lids heavy, she closed her eyes.

"Now there's a Kodak moment if I ever saw one." Mike groaned. "Gorgeous women curled up like a pile of puppies."

Devon couldn't believe she'd just about drifted off. She started to sit up. A warm hand pressed her shoulder against the netting. *Neil.* With one touch, she knew it was him. Her body arched toward the contact while she searched with the other hand for James. He wouldn't be far behind his boyfriend.

At the same time, Dave reached for Kayla, settling her closer to where he'd climbed onto his masterpiece.

"Stay. Please." Neil crawled beside her, tucking her against the furnace of his chest.

"Mmm. Toasty." Devon didn't flinch when he rolled, presenting her to James. The other man sandwiched her between them, infusing her shoulders, ass and the back of her thighs with a twin blast of heat.

The ropes shifted as Mike and Joe joined the fray. A gorgeous tangle of limbs and sleek, toned bodies littered the expanse. They paired off and spread out a little—

enough to be comfortable, but not so far that they added unnecessary space.

"Look, I don't say this enough…" Mike stole the opportunity to address them while they studied the deep royal blue of the twilight sky. "I can't imagine my life without you all. Without this connection we have. The wedding is coming up quick, and I believe I'm the luckiest bastard in the whole world. Honestly. I do."

Joe rumbled from beside them, where he cuddled Morgan against his chest. "Why do I sense and enormous *but*?"

"It's true." Mike sighed. "I'm worried, for the first time since we found each other, that if we're not honest now, we could lose this closeness. I refuse to let us drift apart."

Devon felt like an interloper. Hell, she'd barely gotten to know them and they were a decade into their friendship. "Should I go?"

"Shh." Neil put his hand over her mouth.

"Hell no, you shouldn't leave." Dave rounded on her. "He's talking to you too. You're part of us. Can't you sense it? This crazy bond? It's happened to us enough times now to recognize when we meet someone that belongs here. It doesn't take long to be sure. Unless you don't sense it?"

She bit her lip until Neil removed his fingers to let her speak. "There's a connection."

"That's good enough for me." Mike shifted, rising to his knees so they could see him better. "I'm telling you right now that I trust you. Each and every one. If something were to happen to me, I'm confident you would look after Kate."

She whimpered beside her soon-to-be-husband.

"Don't worry, babe. I'm not planning on checking out anytime soon. But why should it be any different when we're here? Now. Together. I love you, Kate. Same as Joe does Morgan and Dave with Kayla. Neil, James and Devon too. Being with the crew before we met you didn't impact that. Changing how we act around each other is stifling us. I'm afraid it will lead to fights. To discontent." He rubbed his temples. "I've been thinking about it a lot lately. I'm more sure now than ever that how we've gone about things is not the answer. Watching and staying apart sucks. We need to be together. It's how we're best. However feels natural. Right, Kayla?"

"It makes sense to me, yes." She roused from Dave's embrace. "If you want to express your affection physically, you should. Like the other day. I could tell when Dave walked through the door. His eyes were brighter and he hugged me twice as hard as usual. It's a vital part of you guys. Sharing like that. Whatever seems right and nothing else. But I expect you to tell me all about it, in detail, if I'm not there to enjoy it firsthand."

Murmurs from around the group ensured they were all in agreement.

Devon shivered. "If I had a vote, I would love to watch you do more than play voyeurs. As hot as things got the other day, I saw you struggling to stay detached and I wondered... God, you have no idea the dreams I've had the past two nights."

"You *do* have a say." Mike nodded at her. "Each of us does. I'm guessing we'd all be in favor of sharing that link with each other. With you."

A smattering of curses, moans and pleas—both masculine and feminine—filled the wild evening. Rice-paper lanterns with botanical prints cast a soft glow over the gathering. Radiance enveloped them as darkness gathered outside the boundaries of their intimate world. Nothing beyond the reach of their spell mattered.

James moaned and Neil caressed her shoulder. "Sort of like your first time all over again."

"Unless you count fantasies, group sex is definitely something new for me." She smiled up at him, accepting his light kiss.

"We'll be gentle. At least where you're concerned." Mike grinned. He didn't hesitate in resuming his usual role, foreman through and through. "James. Get on your hands and knees in the middle of us. Let's see how well Dave designed this contraption."

CHAPTER FIVE

he men surrounded the slightest member of their group, staying low and helping him stabilize while they caused ripples in the surface of the lounger. If the presence of four smoking hot men and their fantastic ladies messed with James's equilibrium as much as it did hers, Devon understood his need for their steadying touch.

The women followed their guys until one couple occupied each side of the square rope-work. It then resembled a dirty version of *Hungry, Hungry Hippos* with James in imminent danger of having his marbles devoured. *There* was a game that had taught major life lessons... Slam the handle—as hard and fast as possible—over and over and over until somebody wins. No wonder it had been her favorite.

The adult jungle gym turned out to be great for more than relaxing. They could indulge their creativity. James spread his legs. Pliable cords, set close enough that he didn't have to worry about sinking through, supported each of his knees.

What was the rope made out of? It was soft enough to be silk. She'd ask the crew later.

Much later.

James's knuckles went white as they wrapped around one of the strands that created perfect grips. Spaced at frequent intervals, they ensured no matter what height he was, there would have been a rung guaranteed to be comfortable.

"Simple and ingenious." She didn't realize she'd spoken aloud until Dave answered her.

"Thanks, Dev."

"The possibilities are endless," Kate murmured as though she contemplated a thousand or so positions she'd like to experiment with.

"We have all the time in the world to try whatever you can concoct," Joe chimed in, making James groan.

"Speak for yourself. If someone doesn't touch me soon I'm going to die." He attempted to rub his crotch, but tipped.

Mike righted him, chuckling at James's plight.

"Diabolical." The smaller man shook his head. "I should have known."

"So, how are you going to convince Joe to stroke your cock for you?" Mike's inquiry turned squeaky at the end. It took Devon a second to notice Kate's arm had snaked around his hip from behind him to fondle *his* package. Devon couldn't help but stare as his cock thickened, overflowing his fiancée's palm.

"I'll blow him." James didn't sound like he minded. In fact, it kind of came out like begging.

"I'm sure he'd appreciate that. Fair trade, Joe?"

"Yeah. I want him to get me nice and hard for Morgan." He angled his head to steal a red-hot kiss from his lady.

"After watching James working your hard-on I might not need you to fuck me." She panted when he released her lips.

"I'll always need you, Morgan." The intensity of his stare seemed to melt his future wife.

Devon could relate. She didn't think before sidling closer to Neil. His abs scorched her hands when she rested her palms on the flexing muscles.

"Mmm."

"If you really want to rev him up, rub his chest." James tossed the hint over his shoulder in her direction.

"No fair, tag-teaming me like that." Neil groaned when Devon massaged his pecs, pausing to flick her thumbnails over his hard nipples. "Ah. Damn."

James's chuckle was short lived. Joe scooted tighter in front of James and fed the kneeling man his erection. Their lover obliged greedily, sucking the shaft down to the base in one fluid slurp.

"I have a plan," Mike announced. "We're going to play spin the construction worker. Whoever his mouth points to wins the BJ lottery. If you're on his right, you'll work his cock. I think the person in the rear can figure out something that suits you both."

"What about the guy on the left?" Dave, currently in that position, actually raised his hand, making Devon and several others laugh out loud.

"That lucky bastard will fuck his woman. When he makes her come, we'll turn James ninety degrees. Not one second sooner."

Mike grinned, clearly pleased with himself when Joe slowed James's sucking with a light tap on his cheek. "And if James can hold out until each of our girls has come at least once, we'll make sure he gets a special prize. Whatever he requests. Sound like fun?"

"Hell, I'm halfway to orgasm thinking about it." Kayla shifted beside Dave. She rubbed her thighs together, drawing Devon's attention to the glimmer of arousal coating the tops of them.

James paused his sensual assault on Joe's cock. "I know what I want."

"Yeah? What?" Joe painted moisture over James's lips with the tip of his cock.

"I want all of the guys to fuck me, to come on me. It's been almost a year since..." He trailed off.

Kate petted his flank from her position at his side. "I'm sorry, James. You should have said something sooner. I wouldn't have kept Mike to myself if I had understood how you missed him. All of you."

Devon didn't realize she'd held her breath until Neil cupped her hand in his and whispered over his shoulder, "Are you ready for this? There won't be any stopping them soon."

"You could say that." From her position, crouched behind him, she ground her mound against his hip.

He growled and captured her mouth in a brief yet fierce kiss. When he relented, her eyes fluttered open once more. Mike had shifted closer, reaching beneath James to cup his balls and stiffening shaft. Kate hugged the foreman from behind, kissing his back and studying the motions of his roaming hand.

James moaned and spread his legs wider, arching his back. The motion presented his ass to her and Neil.

"Hang on a sec." Dave lunged for the edge of the net and jabbed his hand into the plants surrounding one of the supports. He retrieved something then tossed it to Neil, who caught it effortlessly in one palm.

"Dude, did you pluck this from the lube bush?" Neil laughed as he uncapped the small bottle.

"Always prepared, you know." Dave wiggled his eyebrows. "I stashed some supplies earlier, just in case."

"I'm not sure what merit badge you get for this, but nice work." Neil grimaced. "I don't suppose you have some condoms over there too, do you?"

Devon tapped Neil's elbow. When he glanced at her, she whispered, "I'm on the pill. You don't have to if..."

"We're clean. All of us." Neil groaned. "Are you sure?"

"Yeah." She bit her lip.

Neil groaned. He tried twice to open the bottle before he drizzled the gel over his fingers. Some dripped off, landing on James's exposed ass.

The kneeling man twitched, dislodging Joe's cock from his mouth long enough to beg, "Hurry, Neil. Mike's still fucking amazing at hand jobs."

"You always did like his technique. A little rougher than the rest of us, huh?" Neil painted the lubrication over James's ass, notching the tip of one finger at his clenched hole.

Devon inched closer for a better view. She allowed her hands to cruise over her body. They soothed the flames licking at her chest and pussy as she observed the guys— whom she'd come to respect on the job— transform into versions of themselves so much more primal and honest than the reserved shells they'd donned before.

"Amazing." She scanned the men and women ringing James. They were focused on his pleasure and their own. Nothing so powerful had ever graced her life. Privileged to be among them, she abandoned any reservations and soaked in the raw passion they created together.

"Yes, you are." Neil kissed her without slowing the steady penetration of his finger into his lover's ass. With his free hand, he cupped her breast, rolling the pad of his thumb over her hardened peak.

A cry from her left drew her attention. She looked over in time to see Dave finish burying himself in Kayla. He blanketed her long, strong body, shuddering when she wrapped her arms and legs around him, drawing him closer to her center.

A spasm clenched Devon's pussy. She had to avert her eyes or risk coming right then. Except every place her greedy gaze landed, it feasted on another treat. Joe threw his head back, exposing the cords of his neck to Morgan's nibbles as he began to rock into James's mouth. Kate had lowered herself to her back to reward Mike for his dexterous hands by laving his cock and balls with slow laps of her tongue.

Devon couldn't stop herself. She reached down and took hold of Neil's erection, which strained against his six-pack abs. She fisted him despite his groan and his attempts to convince her to let go.

"I won't last if you do that." He bit her lower lip then soothed the sting with flicks of his tongue.

"You'd better." Mike gritted his teeth. "No disappointing your lady, unless you're hoping another crew member will pick up your slack."

The threat alone was enough to weaken Devon's legs. If she hadn't already been kneeling, she would have crashed to the netting.

"Fuck, no." Neil snapped. He pumped his finger deep into James's clenching hole, adding a second digit when the man in front of them rocked back, asking for more.

"Dave, you'd better not dally," Mike called out orders. "I'm sure you can push Kayla over the edge faster than that."

The woman's response was unintelligible. However, the trails left by her neat nails as they scratched down her lover's back spoke volumes. Dave's hips ground against his girlfriend's, escalating her whimpers to full out cries in less than a minute.

"There you go, Kay." Neil encouraged her. "Open your eyes. Watch what you two are doing to us."

When the naturist peeked from beneath the shadow of her enthusiastic lover, she groaned. Her arm flailed out, grasping onto James's wrist where it supported him. She shivered violently as she inspected Joe's shaft tunneling between James's generous lips. Then she scanned to Mike's impressive manipulation. When she observed Neil preparing his lover for the rest of the crew, she lost it.

"Oh, Dave," she whimpered. "I want you to fuck him like you're fucking me. Hard. Relentless. Perfect."

"Shit." Dave's hips hitched in their fluid stride. "Don't talk like that, Kay, or I won't make it. You're so fucking hot. So tight. So wet. Jesus."

"Tell me." Kayla drew him to her for a kiss, eliminating the possibility of him responding for long seconds.

"Yeah. Fuck." He grunted. "I'm going to ride him for you, baby. You want to see it, don't you? Me feeding my cock into his tight ass?"

Poor Kayla. Devon shuddered as her new friend succumbed to the sexy verbal assault. Hell, when Neil pressed two fingers inside Devon's soaked pussy, she almost joined their host in her epic climax.

Dave roared, making Devon wonder if he hadn't spilled inside the sultry woman writhing beneath him. When Kayla quieted, he sat up, resting on his haunches, his fingers clamped around the base of his massive hard-on like a poor man's cock ring.

"Nice work." Mike's praise lowered an octave or two from his usual tone. "I didn't think you stood a chance there."

Dave grimaced, his cock still throbbing with every beat of his heart. He took several deep breaths then nuzzled Kayla, bringing her back to reality gently. She whispered to him, too quiet for the rest to hear then kissed him so tenderly Devon wasn't surprised to find tears prickling her eyes.

Kay patted her guy on the cheek. She relaxed into the netting. Dave tucked one of the blankets over her then smiled. "I love you."

"Love you too," she murmured. "Now run along and play. I think James is ready for you."

"Who cares about James?" Morgan drew chuckles with her false dismissal. "I need Joe to fuck me. Now. Enough teasing."

Neil squirted another generous dollop of lube onto James's ass, making sure to incorporate it before withdrawing his fingers. He smacked the cute bubble butt then nudged James's hip, encouraging him to turn. Devon loved how Neil supported James, helping him into his new position, rubbing his ankles and knees to keep the blood circulating.

While James concentrated on giving Joe's cock one final kiss goodbye then welcoming Mike into his mouth, Neil reached over to Dave. He wrapped his hand around his partner's cock and slicked the shaft, though it already bore the remnants of Kayla's pleasure. Neil wouldn't take any chances with his lovers' comfort. That much was clear.

"Go slow." Neil guided Dave to James. "You're a lot thicker than me, and it's been a while since he's had anyone else."

"You might have thought about that before Mike let me fuck Kayla. You know nothing turns me on more. Unless it's this. I can't believe we're doing this again. That she's watching. All of you are."

So much for restraint. Dave fisted his hands at his sides and pressed forward.

Mike withdrew his cock from James's mouth. "Watch your teeth, kid."

"Hard when he's splitting me open." James's back heaved as Dave attempted to seat himself.

Neil nuzzled James's shoulder, whispering in his ear. He rubbed his boyfriend's back.

Devon couldn't stop herself. If she could make this better for James, she would. She crept up next to Neil and placed her left hand over the base of James's spine. She soothed him as best she knew how, dropping light kisses to the concave dip above his ass.

"If you stroke him, it'll help him enjoy this." Neil advised her.

Devon ran her right hand from James's ribs over his flat belly, admiring the contours of his svelte muscles. She arrowed south until her fingers bumped into his semi-erect dick. Then she explored. Soft skin, heavy balls, his firming shaft—everything about him intrigued her.

"There you go, James," Dave crooned, wrapping his hands around James's trim hips. He held James in place as he applied steady, unrelenting pressure with the tip of his cock on the smaller man's stretching hole. "Almost have me. Think how amazing it'll be when I'm in you all the way."

"Ah. Yes." James's head hung between his shoulders. "Do it. Now."

Devon began a gentle tug on James's cock. It expanded in her fist, forcing her to loosen her grip and travel farther on every pass to stroke the entire length. When the head of Dave's erection poked through the last resistance of James's ass the guys moaned in unison.

James cried out. Pain, pleasure or both, she couldn't say for sure.

"That's so damn hot." Kayla cheered them on from where she curled on her side behind the action. If Devon guessed right, the other woman touched herself beneath the blanket.

"Let me see." Joe sat up far enough on the other side of James to get an eyeful. "Shit, yes. Fuck him good, Dave. Open him up for me. I want to ride him hard."

"Me first." Morgan settled herself in her fiancé's lap, reverse cowgirl style. She faced the group as she lowered herself onto the stiff flesh jutting from Joe's crotch. Devon increased the pace of her stroking. She imagined how good it would feel to be filled right now. Joe's cock disappeared inside Morgan until her pussy rested on his balls.

Dave must have enjoyed the abandon on Morgan's face as much as Devon did. He began to move with long, careful glides until he fused his abdomen to James's ass.

"Feel better?" Mike wrapped his fingers in James's hair and guided the smaller man's mouth back to his cock. "Yeah, damn. That's what I thought."

James devoured Mike.

The foreman wrapped one arm around his soon-to-be wife and tugged her close to his side. He bent down to suck on her breast as another man serviced him. Kate stared. She reached out, tracing one finger around the girth of Mike's cock, which was surrounded by James's supple lips. Her wandering hands ended up pillowing Mike's balls as they swung against James's chin.

Neil turned his attention to Devon, nodding to where she had pumped steel into James's flagging erection. "You have that covered?"

"I think so."

James moaned his agreement and fucked into her grasp.

"Good." Neil smiled. He surprised her by sliding to her rear. "I guess that means I'm free to play with you instead."

Her head lolled onto his shoulder when he bracketed her from behind. His long fingers skimmed down her front from her breasts to her abdomen. He paused over her mound, drawing lazy circles on the sensitive skin there. When she whimpered, James tensed. His whole-body flex wrung corresponding groans from Dave and Mike.

"Joe, you better be doing your best with Morgan over there." Neil laughed, buffeting strands of Devon's hair. "I can already tell these two are riding the edge."

Morgan shrieked, confirming his suspicions. Joe hammered into her from below, all of them focused on the guys who formed the centerpiece of their lascivious display.

"And how about you?" Neil sucked hard on Devon's neck. "I can't believe how wet you are."

She sought his teasing fingers with her pussy, painting his hand with her arousal.

"By the time it's your turn, you'll combust with one stroke." Neil didn't do much to preserve her self-control. "Ever come from a man sliding inside you before?"

Hell, she wasn't going to make it that long if he kept this up.

"Joe!" Morgan cried out as she bounced on his lap. She made the motion look effortless and graceful as she swung her hips, tracing a sinuous glide path on every pass.

"Yes." Her mate molded his hands to her breasts, pinching the hard nipples. "Come for me. For us."

Dave yanked his cock from James's ass. As Morgan mewled and arched impossibly in Joe's hold, the first splash of Dave's come jetted onto James's back. The moment the warm line of sticky fluid branded James's skin, his cock pulsed in Devon's grip.

"Not yet." She removed her hand. "I want you to come with us."

He whimpered, already spinning so that his ass aimed toward Joe. Morgan untangled herself from her fiancé, collapsing onto one of the puffy pads Kayla had made and grabbing another blanket to settle in for the rest of the show.

Joe didn't waste any time. He sprang forward, causing a wave to roll through the rest of the net, impacting them all. They leaned on each other, finding support and mutual longing waiting.

Devon twisted to the side to make room for Neil to approach James's mouth with his cock, but the man behind her prevented her from moving. "You'd better take my turn, sweetheart. No way can I let him suck me now."

"Is that okay?" She looked instinctively to Mike.

"Whatever feels right, Dev."

She glanced down at James. His startlingly familiar eyes seemed enormous in the low light. He reached for her. She went. "You're sure?"

"Mmm. Yes, please." He waved his fingers, motioning for Neil to position her closer. Neil wrapped her in his strong arms. She rested on his tight, muscular chest so she didn't have to sacrifice the view of Joe plunging into James's ass.

Over and over.

Harder and harder.

James nudged her thighs wide apart then buried his face in her moist lips. He flicked his tongue around her opening then up to her clit. Every thrust Joe made into James's ass shoved James's lips tight against her swollen pussy. And yet she needed more. Needed to be filled. Fucked. Joined together with one of these phenomenal men.

Like Kate, who lay on her side, facing the main attraction while Mike pumped into her from behind. He held her knee up high in one hand, opening her impossibly for his savage fucking. She slipped one hand down her torso. Her fingers flashed ultra-quick over her clit.

Devon whimpered as she considered how good that would feel. She fought the current lifting her toward orgasm, wanting to hold out for the ultimate merger. Just when she thought she wouldn't make it, Joe froze. He rammed inside James once, twice more before pulling out and spilling his seed all over the swell of James's ass.

"You were supposed to wait for Katiebug." Neil *tsked*.

There was no need to be worried. Kate screamed, bucking in Mike's strong grasp as Joe painted the last strands of his release over James's soft skin. Mike bit Kate's neck, slowing his frantic thrusts as she glided down the far side of ecstasy. Morgan handed Kate a pillow and a blanket. Then she lifted the edge of the nest she'd made to invite her lover into the warmth she'd generated for him.

Mike impressed Devon. He rose to his knees after one final sweet kiss on Kate's forehead. He was controlled yet powerful when he advanced inside James. Dave should have been up for occupying James's mouth next. However, he seemed loathe to leave the comfort of the spot where he snuggled with Kayla.

They redefined the rules to accommodate the needs of the remaining players.

"I have to fuck you, Dev," Neil growled as he pressed her back to the rope mesh. He smothered her body in welcoming heat. She strained her neck, attempting to connect with James and see how he responded to Mike's expert loving.

"Help him, Dave." Kayla nudged her boyfriend toward James while she angled herself closer to Devon and Neil. "Here, watch them."

Devon didn't flinch when Kayla used her body to prop up Devon. Her head was pillowed on the other woman's chest. Lush and inviting. Devon closed her eyes and lost herself in sensation, untroubled by false boundaries or the labels people would try to apply to what they shared here tonight. None of those stigmas mattered. She opened her heart and allowed the experience to take her where it would.

"You look so sexy together." Neil sighed as he stroked first Kayla's hair, then Devon's. He settled in the V of her thighs, rocking his erection over her saturated pussy. "I have to have you."

"She's trembling." Kayla chaffed Devon's arms as though it were cold making her system go haywire. Too bad there was no cure for sensual devastation. Then again, if this was what it felt like to be sick she never would hunt for a cure.

"Please." Devon couldn't muster anything more intelligent than that. She feared if he didn't possess her soon, she'd come with the next breeze over her clit.

"You're pretty when you beg." He flashed her a wolfish smile as he fit them together and pushed.

"No. No." She tried to shove him off when she realized that his invasion would mean surrender, but Kayla's hands kept her arms pinned by her side. "Not yet."

"I told you I'd make you come with one stroke, didn't I?" His arrogant grin stole her last shred of resistance.

Devon shattered around him as he advanced down her channel, battling the tight rings of muscle contracting in rhythmic cycles. Instead of slowing, he ramped up his attack. A quick, harsh explosion of rapture turned into something she'd never experienced before. The peak of her climax extended. It picked up again and again the moment she thought it might flag.

"That's right, Dev." Kayla combatted the fire in her skin with gentle caresses. "Let go. Let him push you further than you've ever gone before."

"Oh, shit." Mike grunted. "It's too much."

Devon saw arcs of his pearly come shoot from his cock to drape over James's ass and pool in his lower back. The proof of their leader's satisfaction seemed to be too much for James. He shouted a warning. Joe continued to milk James's cock.

"You earned it, James." Dave held the kneeling man as he surrendered. Neil's hips stuttered as he allowed his glance to stray to his lover.

"Give it to him, James. All of it. No holding back." The animalistic command from Neil had Devon clamping down on him again… No, still.

James spilled his release over Joe's hand, which pumped him dry. Unlike the other guys, he didn't relax or cuddle with his spent crewmates. Instead, James crawled closer until he joined her and Neil where Neil still pummeled her.

The power of so many hot stares on her ratcheted Devon to new heights. A foreign pressure built low in her belly. From an endless orgasm, something new and bright developed. It glowed stronger, hotter, inside her when James knelt between Neil's spread legs. He put one hand on each cheek of Neil's ass and spread him wide.

If James hadn't just sprayed Joe's hand with enough force to sandblast Joe's skin, she might have thought he planned to fuck Neil while Neil fucked her. Oh God. Then he did something she didn't expect. His tongue slithered from between his lips and rimmed Neil's ass.

The cock buried inside her jerked as though someone had touched it with a live wire. Neil cursed, held perfectly still for half a second then went wild. He fucked her with an innate grace that complimented his complete surrender to base instinct. James dipped his tongue inside the clenching portal of his lover's ass, fucking it even as he wriggled the wet muscle all around.

The knot of tension drew tighter inside Devon until she feared falling from so great a height. Could she survive the drop?

Neil lifted his head, staring straight into her eyes. "Need. You. Now."

She whimpered because she couldn't give him what he craved. The power of their exchange frightened her away from the edge. He fucked harder, the ridges of his veined shaft stroking her in all the right places. James increased the frequency of his devious manipulation.

"We've got you, Devon." Kayla smiled down at her. "I won't let you fall."

The relief that suffused her made her reach without thinking. Devon wrapped her fingers around the back of Kayla's neck and tugged. She accepted the warmth her friend offered in a gentle, grounding kiss that rocked her foundation.

"Oh Jesus." Neil gasped. "So damn hot. I'm coming."

She didn't need his warning to know that. Liquid fire seared her insides as jet after jet of his come overflowed her pussy. James sank from his attentions on Neil's ass to lap at the excess. He nuzzled Neil's tight sac and feasted on the creamy result of their loving.

Between the silky press of Kayla's lips on her mouth, Neil's body and cock imprinting on her core and James's tongue lapping at the seam between them, Devon lost control. She came so hard she thought she might injure Neil. His agonized moan seemed ripped from his chest as she squeezed him again and again and again.

She exploded in an orgasm strong enough to trigger an out of body experience. She could see her toes curling around one of the silken strands of the net, watched herself getting lost in the arms of a man and woman she had met not long ago but could never again be separated from.

Devon reached for James, unable to find him in the sea of pleasure and light that consumed her. She searched as far down Neil's back as she could reach, longing to complete the circuit by linking her fingers with James.

He wasn't there.

As though dunked in ice water, she cooled rapidly. Neil crashed to the woven lounger beside her, huffing as though he'd run a marathon. She stroked his still flexing ass as she scanned the area wildly for the other man who'd given her pleasure.

A mop of unruly brown hair disappeared behind the hedge.

Devon would have scrambled out of the netting, less than gracefully, still trying to coordinate her limbs. Except Neil clung to her, smiling against her breast as though he hadn't noticed James missing.

"We need to find—" Her warning cut short when Dave pitched his voice above the sighs and soft whispering of the other couples. They groaned when the beefcake jostled them all by rolling to the edge of the lounger where he plucked something from one of the pretty flowerbeds surrounding one of the corner supports.

No more lube needed, Davey.

He returned, tugging Kayla to his side.

"I realize this might be the most unorthodox time for this, but like you always say...it feels right." He cupped Kayla's cheek in fingers that looked far too large for how gently he touched her. "You and me. We're permanent. This. You. I need it forever. Please tell me you do too, Kay."

He cracked open a small velvet box and withdrew a ring featuring a rock large enough to glitter even in the diffuse lighting from the lanterns.

"Is that—?" She sat bolt upright.

"Yeah." He grinned at her slack jaw. "Will you marry me?"

Things kicked into slow motion right about then. Devon's heart expanded as Kayla's eyes filled with joyous tears. She smiled when Kay flung herself at her sturdy lover, squealing.

Dave reached for her at the same time.

Somewhere in the middle, their limbs collided and the ring pinched between

Dave's banged-up thumb and forefinger popped into the air. It flipped end over end, sending a cascade of rainbows across the wide-eyed faces around the couple, before splashing into the pond below them with a distinct *plop*.

"Oh shit." Neil tried to muffle his laughter against Devon's shoulder.

Mike reacted first. "Don't freak. It's all right. This is a closed system, we'll wait until morning and then fish it out nice and easy."

"Morning?" Kayla framed her face with her palms. "Oh no. I'm so sorry—"

"My fault. I came so hard I almost blew the top of my fucking skull off. Then when you kissed Devon... Christ. My fingers aren't working quite right." Dave groaned. "It fell right through the ropes. I heard the splash."

"So did I." Neil already scanned the space below them. Aside from the occasional glint off a ripple on the surface, the rest was inky blackness.

Dave looked around at his friends. "This is going to be funny one day, right?"

"It's cracking me up right now." Neil smiled.

"I thought I was following my gut. Maybe I had gas from all those baked beans." Dave *thunked* his forehead with the heel of his hand. "She didn't say yes, did she?"

"Start over." Mike suggested. "We'll worry about the ring in a minute."

Dave took a huge breath. "Kayla. I think tonight proved everything I already knew. I've found the only place I want to be. The only people I want to share my life with. I wanted to ask you to accept the ring I dropped in the motherfucking koi pond as a symbol of our love. I wanted to know… Will you marry me?"

Kayla squealed again and tackled Dave.

They tumbled to the lounger in a knot of arms and long, tattooed legs.

Coming to rest on his back, Dave held Kayla's hips as she straddled him. "Is that a yes?"

"Yes!" Half the crew shouted the answer at the same time as Kayla.

Tears poured down Devon's face. It was the most beautiful moment she'd ever witnessed. Goof and all.

The guys kicked into action, making arrangements to pull lights off their trucks and haul a battery down to power them.

"I'm the smallest. I'll go in once you guys grab the gear. It shouldn't be hard to find if I can slip under the edge there. Dave and Kayla stay where you are so I have a reference point."

She shouldn't have bothered with that directive. The couple didn't appear to be moving anytime soon. They cuddled, lost in each other and the pure love they shared.

***

Devon rounded a bend in the path, planning to run up to the driveway and retrieve the waterproof flashlight she'd recalled she'd stashed in her glove compartment. She jogged up the hillside, grateful for the warmth her muscles and lingering adrenaline generated.

Harsh voices caught her off guard and she slowed.

"Why are you being such a dickhead?" Neil's frustration sliced through the night. She couldn't be sure, but she thought he might have shoved his lover, who appeared to be ignoring the aggravated man.

This time her tremor had nothing to do with the cold, unless it was the frost in Neil's tone.

Guess he'd found James. She started to turn around and leave them to their privacy.

"You made love to Devon." James sounded both admiring and wrecked if such a thing were possible.

The agony in his proclamation had her longing to wrap him in a hug though she was probably the last person he'd welcome comfort from. Torn, she couldn't walk away yet she didn't dare to intrude.

"I've fucked dozens of women while you watched. You never minded before. All of a sudden this is a problem?" Neil didn't cut him any slack. "You know what I need. Hell, you've gotten off on sharing plenty before."

"You've never looked at a woman the way you look at her. You've never fit with one of them like you were meant for each other." James's voice cracked.

Whoa. Devon couldn't justify hiding in the shadows a moment longer. She emerged into the open meadow, approaching them as carefully as if they were an improperly braced structure. "How exactly does Neil look at me?"

They turned toward her with matching frowns.

"Like he looks at *me*." James shook his head. "Looked at me. Like you're everything to him. I never cared about playing around before because I could tell his exchanges with women were purely physical. This is the first time he's really taken a lover. I guess I assumed it'd always be me he went home with at the end of the day."

"I'm not trying to change that." Devon's heart ached. Because somewhere deep down she could admit she was lying. She wanted Neil. Tonight. Every night. Forever. She should have known whatever unconventional role she'd been playing was too good to be true.

"It's too late. Has been since the very first day. When I found you on the curb, he'd already fallen. I could see it in his eyes." James shrugged. "You didn't do anything but be you. I want to be pissed, but I can't. He loves you. And I can see why. You're sweet, strong, funny, hardworking, sexy and kind. Just promise me you'll treat him well. I won't stand for him to be hurt."

Neil interrupted. "James, what are you saying?"

"I'm going to grant your wish. I've only ever wanted you to be happy." James bit his lip to still the quivering there.

"He wants you." Devon had never been surer of anything in her life.

"No, he wants *you*." James didn't scrub the tear that ran down his cheek.

She leaned closer, opening her arms.

James spun away.

Before she could follow, Mike and Joe crashed up the path, laughing and causing a ruckus. "What's taking so long? Dave's getting his panties in a bunch."

Devon shrugged and left the men alone. Maybe Neil could talk to his boyfriend if she gave them peace.

***

Two hours later, Devon held the ring in her fist and pumped it over her head while doing a silly victory dance. Dave and Joe stared at her tits for a second or two before hauling her from the pond.

"I believe this belongs to you." She placed the gorgeous hunk of diamond and platinum in Dave's broad palm.

"No, ma'am. It belongs to her." He knelt at Kayla's feet and slid the ring onto her shaking third finger. "I love you, Kay."

"I love you too." She sniffled. "It's gorgeous, Dave. Truly."

"Not half as much as you." He climbed to his feet and kissed her temple before turning to Devon.

"Thank you." They both enveloped her in a hug despite the rivulets of pond water dripping off her. "Oh, no. You're freezing."

Mike and Kate swooped in with blankets to wrap her in, though even a blowtorch couldn't combat the ice solidifying her heart. She stood on the fringes of the gathering as the rest of the crew celebrated. Neil pulled James into a fierce hug. Sometime during the search, their tempers had dissipated.

Neil kissed the slighter man full on the mouth. Their lips slanted, interlocking. They got lost in each other. No way would she risk destroying that bond.

Devon backed slowly into the shadows, outside the glow bathing the rest of the crew.

When she was sure they hadn't noticed, she ran.

Toward her forgotten dress.

Toward the keys to her truck.

Toward her lonely reality—one that didn't involve a fantasy come to life in the form of two hot studs and an array of loyal, lifelong friends.

When she crested the hill, dragging the blankets through the grass behind her, Devon's shoulders slumped. Neil and James leaned against their truck as though they'd used their dynamic duo powers to leap up the hillside in a single bound.

"How—?"

"Not important." James crossed his arms over his chest.

"Where do you think you're going like that?" Neil surveyed her from her damp hair to her bare, painted toes.

"Home." She hated how her teeth chattered.

"Our home, sure." James relaxed his stance, opening his arms. "I'm sorry you overheard us arguing before. I didn't mean to scare you off."

"Does that mean your feelings have changed?" She allowed herself to lean on him, no matter how weak it made her. His arms came around her. He was so generous considering the depth of the despair she'd glimpsed in him earlier.

"Why don't we talk about that when we're not all exhausted and hypothermia is less of a possibility?" He evaded her questions, killing her with kindness.

"He's right, Dev." Neil opened the door to their truck and ushered them inside before rounding to the driver's side. He trapped her between them. "Let's figure things out in the morning."

James cranked up the heat and sang softly to her while he rocked them both. Before they'd made it out of the driveway, her lids were unbearably heavy.

CHAPTER SIX

From the doorway of the walk-in closet he shared with his boyfriend, James's peripheral vision treated him to a glimpse of Neil exiting the shower. He refused to stare though Neil ruffled his hair with a thick gray towel, and then slung it low around his waist. The dreamy smile he wore as he sank to the edge of their bed beside Devon looked even finer on him than the tux he'd rented for Mike and Kate's wedding. And that was saying something.

James couldn't bear to spend the night pretending not to notice such blatant gooeyness. He reached for the duffel he'd packed and stashed beneath the neat row of the few button up shirts he owned. After tugging on a fitted T-shirt, he slipped the strap of the bag crosswise over his chest.

He rehearsed his departure announcement several times before he shut the door behind him, determined to keep calm.

A deep breath didn't do him any good when he spun around and caught the pale, hollow cast to Neil's cheeks, devoid of the dimples he'd so recently sported. Air lodged in James's throat, choking him. Still, he managed to spit out his decision. "Gonna bunk over at Joe and Morgan's tonight."

"Are you leaving me?" Neil tried to stand. He lost his balance and plopped onto the mattress once more. The gap in his towel wrap widened.

For once, the flash of bronzed skin didn't entice James. He rubbed the ache in his chest. A heart attack couldn't hurt this much. "I'm giving you room to take what you need."

"I need *you*," Neil whispered.

"You need her too."

Even now, Neil's fingers rubbed the crook of her knee as though he could leech strength from their cute, tomboyish assistant.

"Too. As in *both*. Not one or the other." It sounded as though every syllable cost Neil a year of his life. The scratchy, desperate pleas were foreign territory for James's confident lover.

"Are you sure? Maybe you should spend time alone with her and see." It killed James to offer. But he wouldn't risk what they had by allowing Neil to develop a sliver of regret. It'd be better to sell out on an amazing high than tarnish their gleaming relationship by dragging it through the muck of a prolonged degradation.

"I'm positive." Neil glanced from where Devon had crashed on their bed. Tiny and angelic, she nestled in the chocolate and sky-blue, satin-covered pillows. "Look at her."

James did. He cleared his mind and opened his eyes.

Something in him stirred.

Was that because she was his boyfriend's girlfriend? Or because a spark grew in his gut every time they shared her? Or even hung out with her at work or for fun? Could he remove Neil from the equation and still feel...something...for her?

Women weren't usually his thing. Still, her honest curiosity called to him. He toyed with the overnight bag, lifting it partially over his head before he realized what he was doing.

"And look at you." Neil rose and stepped closer. He framed James's face with gentle hands. "You're so generous. Ridiculously self-sacrificing. A man I wish I could be half as decent as. How can I not want you both? Please, James. Don't make me choose. You. Her. You're perfect. For me. And for each other."

"I—" Some of his doubts evaporated as he stared into the eyes of the only man he'd ever loved so ferociously. Could there be room for another person? Maybe. God knew they had plenty of passion to spare.

"Trust me?" Neil drew the duffle the rest of the way off and kicked it into the corner. He grabbed the hem of James's shirt and dispatched that too.

"I do." James gasped as Neil sank before him, unbuckling his belt then lowering the zipper on his well-worn jeans. "Neil?"

"Yeah?" He looked up from his position on the floor, his lips half an inch from James's cock.

"What are you doing?"

"What do you think?" He licked a trail from James's balls to the tip of his rapidly hardening shaft.

"Did you forget you *hate* giving blow jobs?" As if Neil needed to be reminded of his own dislike. "You don't do it. Not even on my birthday."

"I would do anything for you." Neil serviced James with a tenderness that speared straight to his soul.

James couldn't resist the sublime treat. Within minutes, his knees weakened. Neil braced them on his shoulders as he worshipped the solid hard-on James had for the man he adored. Safe, protected, cherished—James read a dozen promises in the tender ministrations his lover pampered him with.

He tried to prolong the pleasure. Keep it going forever, always knowing that was impossible. Which didn't mean they couldn't revive it again and again. A million times. In each other's arms. As long as he stayed around for Neil to lift him up next time.

With a tortured moan, he poured himself into Neil's hungry mouth.

After drinking every last drop of James's release, Neil led them to their bed. He lay in the center, drawing James with him. One sculpted arm curled around Devon and the other sheltered James. Neil held them both so they rode the ragged rise and fall of his chest.

James listened to the pounding of his mate's heart, so strong he almost missed the ghost of Neil's begging. "Please don't leave us. Please."

"I won't." He couldn't. He'd never be able to walk away without destroying himself in the process. Anything else he'd convinced himself of was a lame combination of bravado and delusion. "I promise. I'm yours."

"Both of ours?"

"We'll see. It's the best I can do." He rubbed the flexing abs he'd often admired until Neil seemed to calm and his respiration evened out.

James lifted his head to study his sleeping boyfriend. After sipping tears from Neil's eyes, he dropped his head to Neil's sturdy shoulder and tried to follow him into sweet dreams.

Despite the exhausting drain of the day and night, he couldn't relax. Restless, he shifted. Devon did too. Her hand covered his on Neil's belly. Delicate fingers wove through his. She sighed, squeezing a little even while unconscious. Rather than being uncomfortable with the gesture, James found the heat of their connection eased him into slumber.

Maybe this could work.

***

Devon's lids fluttered open. She stared across the chiseled expanse of Neil's abdomen, where her cheek rested, to the man occupying the far side of her lover's torso.

Mmm. James. Her other lover. How decadent?

Soft blue light flickered over the slight whisker burn rouging his cheeks. What had she missed by checking out early last night?

A moan rumbled from the chest of the man pillowing them both. Neil's fingers flexed on her ribs as she watched his other hand mirror the pressure on James, hugging them both tighter to him. Devon couldn't muster the energy required to lift her head and check out the television Neil stared at. She murmured, "Are you watching porn?"

James didn't move from his contented slouch. However, the corner of his lips kicked up. "Doubt it. He's not hard. I checked."

"You two know I can hear you, right?"

Her head bounced a little when Neil chuckled. The growl of his stomach almost startled her bolt upright. With one ear pressed to his svelte torso, the rumble echoed louder than a jet engine.

"Oh, yeah. I'm sure now." James blinked then grinned at her. "He's watching the Food Network. Probably *Barbeque University* if I know our boy. I wouldn't be surprised if he came in his pants every time the host gets to the part of the show where he lays on the *crosshatch of grill marks*."

"I'm not wearing pants, smartass." Neil ruffled James's hair. "You know, I wouldn't be forced to drool over another dude's meat if you could cook worth a damn."

"You should be an expert by now. You watch this shit enough." James poked Neil in the stomach. His steely abs didn't dent in a single millimeter.

The pause hung in the air long enough all Devon could do was laugh. "If you're hoping I can channel Rachel Ray, you're out of luck. Sorry, guys. Although, I do have some pretty awesome delivery places programmed into my phone."

She sighed and wondered where they'd stashed her purse.

"No need." Neil snagged a cell off the nightstand and punched in a series of digits from memory. "Do you like chicken lo mein?"

"For breakfast?" Devon raised a brow.

"It's almost noon, sleepyheads." Neil caressed both of their shoulders.

"How long have you been sitting there?" James shifted uneasily.

"About four hours I guess." He shrugged. "The time went by fast. But I really could use something to eat."

"Okay then." Devon grinned. "I *love* chicken lo mein. *If* you order it from Mr. China."

"Wouldn't dare to try anything else." James smiled at her. "We're regulars. Too bad they're pick up only. Give me a minute and I'll get dressed."

"No, I woke you up." Neil untucked himself from their drowsy tangle of limbs. "I'll be back before you know it. Doze off again and I'll help you refuel with steamy, noodley goodness in no time. Or maybe you two could…ah…talk. Or something."

He glanced between them as though they might tear each other limb from limb if he weren't there to referee. Devon laughed. "We'll be fine without a chaperone."

"If only that was my concern." He scrubbed his hand over his sexy scruff.

"You're good?" He shot James a pointed glance.

"Yeah, dad." James and Devon laughed together.

"Fine, fine." Neil flipped them the bird as he hopped into a pair of maroon running shorts and snagged James's discarded T-shirt from the floor. The fitted style, a size smaller than he usually wore, snugged to his muscles. "Don't miss me too much."

They giggled some more until the barking of the neighbor's dog replaced the fading roar of Neil's truck engine, reminding Devon just how alone they really were. "So…"

"So." James covered his face with his palms. "This is horrible. Awkward. All my fault. I'm sorry for yesterday."

Devon hesitated for a moment before reaching out. She nudged his hand from his cheeks and laced their fingers. "That's not necessary. I can't imagine how hard this must be for you. I would be insanely jealous if my boyfriend suddenly had a perma-boner for someone else. Never mind if he introduced them to our relationship. I probably would have walked. After scratching his eyes out with a rusty screwdriver."

"Last night... I'm not proud of it, but I almost did. Walk. Not the gouging thing. That's such a girl move." James grinned as he rearranged the pillows. He rolled to his side so they were eye to eye.

"I realize I'm probably the last person on earth you'd choose to talk to about this. I promise to be open minded if you need to vent. And I meant what I said yesterday, I won't come between you two. What you have is too special. I could leave before he comes back—"

"Don't. You're part of us now." James surprised her by reaching out to prevent her from rising. He traced one of her brows with the tip of his finger. "I admit this is something new for me. Talking. I could get used to having someone to confide in. Neil isn't always the best at emotional frankness."

"Okay, then. I'd like to be totally honest if you'll lend me your ear." She closed her eyes, trying not to purr when he expanded his path above her eye to include her cheek and neck as well.

"I insist." His breath warmed her chin.

She opened her eyes, wondering when they'd drawn so close together.

"If it weren't for you, Neil probably would have scared me away in the beginning. Before I got to know him better. He's a little too...brash sometimes."

"Really?" James considered that for a minute. "I guess I can see that."

"For example, my first day. It was a cluster of an introduction until you came out. Like a translator, you made everything flow between us. You know when to pull him back or when he's skirting my comfort zone. I don't think you realize you temper him."

"Actually, I've always felt like I have to clean up after him when he chows down on those enormous feet of his. I didn't think anyone else noticed." James stared into her eyes, really looking deep for the first time.

Did he see some of himself in her?

"I've noticed a lot about you, James." She narrowed the chasm of remaining space between them, resting her forehead against his. He didn't flinch when she ran her hand up his side, loving the dip and curve of his ribs. "Like how you grit your teeth when someone makes short jokes about you. Or how you take the newspaper to the old lady who lives next door to our project so she doesn't have to struggle down her front stairs every morning. Or how you set aside some of your sandwich meat for that stray cat that's been coming around. Tell Neil you want to adopt it, would you? He can't say no to you. I wouldn't be able to either. It was you I had a crush on first."

"Really?" He seemed so surprised.

"Yes." She dredged courage from the far reaches of her psyche then leaned forward to brush her lips against his. When he opened his mouth, inviting her to take more, she retreated, needing to finish their conversation first. He had to understand. "You're pretty fantastic. And totally my type—loyal, sensitive and smoking hot without trying."

"I'm not usually attracted to women." He tugged a strand of her short hair. "You're not very girly though."

"Gee thanks." Devon barked out a laugh as though the barb hadn't hit a sore spot. "I take back the sensitive part."

"I *like* the way you are." His hand wandered from her face, around the shell of her ear, down her neck then ended up palming her breast. Not that she had much to speak of. Unlike Kate and Morgan. "You're so soft underneath your tough girl act. I'm afraid I'll hurt you."

So was she.

"I never have to worry about that with the crew. They can handle anything I can dish out and then some." His hand skimmed her skin again, this time landing on her ass. He yanked her tight to him, impressing her with the bulge of his cock.

Hallelujah.

"I think I can take you too." She cupped him, savoring the hiss of his intake. "Why don't you try me?"

He nodded almost imperceptibly before gliding his lips over hers with sips lighter than a feather. Something in her unfurled, like a sprouting flower. She knew it would be gorgeous when fully grown. All it needed was the sunshine of his attention and water to fuel the process, which Neil would be happy to supply as the gardener of their affection.

"Damn, Dev." He moaned before sealing their mouths more fully.

Their kiss lingered forever. Playful, intense, exploratory and genuinely affectionate—making out had never meant so much to her. Their flickering tongues communicated more than simple promises.

Her entire body flashed hot when he levered her thigh over his hip. The pressure of his erection riding her slit coupled with the glide of his smooth chest over her nipples as they moved together. Sighing. Smiling. Dancing in time to the synchronized heartbeats that amplified where their bodies converged.

"I want to make love to you, Devon." He groaned against her neck when he retreated to catch his breath. "Not because you're Neil's, but because I think you might be mine too. Will you let me inside you when he comes home?"

"Of course." She squirmed against him, drawing a tortured groan from his delectable throat. "But I don't think I can wait very long. I'm dying to have you."

"Lucky for you both, I'm right here." Neil spoke low enough not to startle them. "Have been for a little while. Couldn't bear to break you apart though."

Her senses went on high alert. She could detect the quickening of James's pulse at the juncture of their torsos. Especially when Neil stalked closer, sliding onto the mattress behind her so she was sandwiched between them both, all three on their sides. The slow, gentle rocking that followed made her pretty sure he stroked himself as he watched her and James continue to grind on one another.

"And for the record, I never expect you to wait. You should do what you like. Make each other happy. Nothing would please me more than to know you're taking care of one another when I'm not around." Neil dropped a kiss to her cheek then squeezed James shoulder. "Go ahead. Forget I'm here."

Devon and James laughed together. As if that were possible.

Still, the prodding of James's cock grew more insistent as he drove it in an arc against her moist folds. Devon didn't suppress the instinct that had her changing the angle of her hips. His blunt tip aligned with her opening.

"You're sure you're ready?" James whispered. "We're not easy men to love. Working together…and the crew…"

"There are a million excuses we could manufacture to quit right now." She silenced his objections with another scorching kiss. When he'd surrendered to the power of their lust, she continued. "I'm not taking the easy path and neither are you. Let's reach for something bigger. Together. All three of us."

"Nine of us," Neil whispered behind her.

"Mmm. Yes." She accepted his refinement.

"Yes." James proved his agreement in the basest method possible. He bored inside her, slow yet steady. His cock seated comfortably in her wet pussy. Being petite had never served her well during sex. Often it became painful. But James fit her just right. He filled her tight channel, gasping her name when he bottomed out.

Neil assisted his lovers by raising Devon's top leg higher, giving James more room to operate. "Go ahead, she's ready for you."

Ready? She might stroke out if he didn't diffuse her skyrocketing blood pressure.

James didn't need to be told twice. He trusted Neil to guide them. The escalating frequency and power of his thrusts inside her didn't mean he abandoned the sweet grind they'd fallen into. No, he combined the two into a rhythm all their own. His pelvis circled her clit at the peak of every driving stroke.

"She's getting tighter." James groaned, his eyes flicking to Neil. "She's going to come on me, isn't she?"

"Damn straight." Neil beamed as he ran his hands all over her shoulders, ass, legs and the breast he could reach. "You're doing good, James. Real good. Make her shatter and I'll take care of you. Show her how much you like being in that pretty pussy."

James stared straight into her eyes.

She knew. Without words. Without sex. He let her see exactly what occupied his soul. She understood because it was the same for her. She'd found her place in the universe. Right here with them. And their friends.

Devon surrendered to the bliss shimmering through her veins and along every nerve ending in her body. She clenched, trying to hold James as deep inside her as he could reside. He cursed as he continued to caress her from the inside, granting every one of her wishes when he kissed her as he pushed her over the edge.

Neil closed in, bracketing her between them, protecting her back from the world outside their group. His cock nudged beside James's. The waves of orgasm built higher as he poked the very tip inside her with his boyfriend's. The unrelenting convulsions of her pussy wouldn't allow him to penetrate completely. Even that little bit was enough to set her off again and again in an unending storm of pleasure filled with chain lighting strikes. Electricity arced between Neil and James, with her conducting the current.

"We'll work up to that, baby." Neil promised. "Someday soon you'll have us both."

James cried out. The desperate shout made her aware he hadn't come with her. Not yet.

"Help him," she begged Neil.

"I thought you'd never ask." He flashed a toothy grin.

When she started to pull away from James, Neil smacked her ass. "Don't you dare. We're going to do this together."

He reached to the nightstand. When the snick of a cap cut through the ringing in her ears, she grinned. "James, you want him to fuck you while you fuck me?"

He grunted, unable to form coherent speech. He followed her as she rolled to her back, spreading her legs wide so he could nestle deep in the V of her thighs. He continued to ride her, less frantically now, prolonging the life of the embers of desire still sparking inside her.

"Fast, Neil. Hard." James tried to tug his boyfriend closer when he approached. A single raised eyebrow from the taller man had James sighing as though turning to putty.

"I'm aiming for slow and gentle." Neil laid a trail of open-mouthed kisses down James's spine. His fingers must have probed James's back entrance. James tensed between her legs and fucked deep. The motion ignited a flare of ecstasy.

"Oh my God." Devon gasped. "I vote for James's idea. Two to one. Hurry, Neil, I think I'm going to come again."

"So responsive." James kissed her until all she could focus on was his taste. Then he grunted.

"Who am I to argue?" Neil fisted his cock in one hand, towering over them as he squatted behind James. With one smooth push, he introduced his hard-on to his lover's ass. "I'll always do my best to give you what you need. Both of you."

He set a demanding pace. Every lunge seated him to the hilt, driving James forward into Devon. The weight of both their lean bodies on her didn't suffocate her. It cocooned her in warmth and security.

"Oh God. Yes. Yes!" James buried his face in the crook of her neck.

Devon speared her fingers into his hair, massaging his scalp.

Neil smiled, slow and broad, as he observed them together. "Thank you. Both of you. I'm the luckiest bastard in the world."

He leaned down to kiss Devon, melting her with the tenderness he showed her lips while fucking them both into oblivion. Then

James titled his face, joining the fray. The instant their tongues tangled, another climax struck.

She unraveled, drawing James with her. The flood of his hot come poured into her pussy. At the same time, Neil shouted and his movements became uneven.

"Ah yeah." James kept coming with spurt after spurt that overflowed her. Moisture trickled along the seam of her ass. She would bet James could say the same if the corded tendons and still pumping hips she saw on Neil were to be believed.

With one last fierce spasm, she hugged James tight. Then they collapsed together. Somehow the guys managed not to crush her as they tumbled to the mattress beside her. Snuggled between their sweaty, heaving chests, she allowed the world to fade away.

But not before she heard them declare their love for each other.

And for her.

EPILOGUE

Devon licked the last of the butter cream icing from her fork one tong at a time. She pretended not to notice the inappropriate stares of her two lovers though she promised herself she'd make up for teasing them later. First, she had a bouquet to catch. Hopefully.

"I can't believe how perfectly everything went off. Most weddings have at least one catastrophe." She scowled. "Then again, I'm wearing a fucking dress. That's pretty horrific."

"You look great. Kate picked something nice for her bridesmaids. Probably since she knows she'll be standing up for Morgan and Kay soon." Neil offered her a bite of his slice of Mike and Kate's wedding cake.

"You don't want it?" She shot him an are-you-crazy glance. "Morgan did an awesome job."

"It's delicious." He agreed. "But watching you devour it is even better."

"I'll give you a dollar if you smuggle us a few slices to eat in bed." James squeezed her knee under the lilac tablecloth. "No utensils needed. I've heard women make pretty great plates."

"Damn. I've always admired the way you think." Neil shot his partner a heated glance. "Although this is wedding cake, not birthday cake."

They laughed together.

Every instant was foreplay for the wedding night that wasn't theirs but might as well have been. Devon glanced up in time to catch Kayla watching them with her head canted as Dave swirled her around the dance floor.

Things had been insane lately as they rushed to wrap up their latest project before Mike left for his honeymoon. The crew hadn't gotten to spend as much time exploring as usual. Could that be why Kay seemed so...interested?

"Guys—?"

"Yeah, Dev?" Neil angled her face toward his to lick a dollop of chocolate from the corner of her mouth.

"Ah, never mind." She shook her head.

"Since when are we keeping secrets from each other?" Neil's intense focus stole her breath.

"Don't let him pressure you." James rubbed her arm. "You don't have to share your thoughts."

"It's more like I'm not sure now is the right time." She surrendered a small sigh. "It's just that I've been wondering lately... How do you know when to act on one of your fantasies with the crew and when you're having an idle daydream?"

"Uh, honey, we've pretty much done everything I ever imagined. Most everything that's possible and a few things I didn't think were." Neil barked out a laugh. "What's left?"

Devon reached for James. He gripped her hand. She peeked up and found Kayla still staring. She met the other woman's gaze and smiled at her friend.

"Do you remember that first night with the whole group?" She looked between her two men, amazed she was so lucky and ashamed of being so greedy.

"You really think I could forget it?" Neil laughed.

"One of the best nights of my life." James bussed her knuckles.

"What about when Kay kissed me?" She couldn't believe heat tingled in her cheeks after all they'd been through.

"Holy shit, Dev." Neil knocked a napkin into his lap when someone passed close behind them. "Are you saying…?"

"Maybe." She shrugged. "I think I'd like to try it. Do you suppose she would—"

"Yes!" Both guys answered in unison.

"Kayla's bi, Devon." James stroked a wisp of hair from her face. "She mentioned it during that snow storm we told you about. The one that finally forced her and Dave to come together."

"Well, then." She cleared her throat. "Maybe next time, when we're all sharing, we could see what happens?"

"Damn, I love you." Neil nibbled a line down her neck while James kissed her sweetly.

"We'll be there with you. No pressure. You know how the crew works." James held her shaking hand. "It gets better every time we're together. And I've noticed lately that some of the girls have wandering hands. It might be time for another crew meeting.

Have you ever wanted to touch the other guys? How would you feel about Kate or Morgan with me or James?"

"Oh." She blinked. "That would be...interesting."

"Interesting hot or interesting not?" Neil didn't pressure her. He seemed genuinely concerned.

"We better talk about this more upstairs. In bed. After someone takes the edge off. Or maybe we could slip under the table here for a minute." She practically panted. "Then I could probably think more clearly."

Both guys laughed.

"Yeah, I feel the same about it." Neil grinned.

"Me too," James echoed.

"Why exactly do you three look like you're up to no good?" Mike sauntered over, his chest puffed up to ridiculous dimensions with his lovely bride on his elbow.

Kate was radiant in her antique lace gown.

"I guess it's because every time I think we can't get luckier, I realize there's more to explore. More love to share." James stood to kiss Kate on the cheek. "I think today's the beginning of a new era. One I can't wait to spend with my best friends."

Morgan and Joe rejoined the head table, a pair of shit-eating grins on their faces. Neil stealthily retucked Joe's shirt while Devon plucked a leaf from Morgan's hair.

"The gardens are lovely, aren't they?" Kate winked.

"Spectacular." Joe nodded, trying to keep a straight face.

The pop song in the background faded into a familiar wedding standard. *What a Wonderful World* had never seemed as perfect to Devon as it did in that moment. The lyrics washed over her as Kayla and Dave took the last two seats at the table.

"Tired of dancing?" Joe poked Dave in the ribs.

"Maybe we missed you guys." Kayla rested her head on Mike's shoulder. "It's going to be weird not having you around for a few weeks."

"Don't let things go to shit. Morgan, you're in charge. Keep these guys in line, would you?" Their foreman chuckled. "I'm going to be too busy to answer calls for bail money."

Kate scooted as close to her husband of three hours as her voluminous crinoline would allow. "You might be the one phoning a friend. I'm pretty sure some of the things I'll be doing to you are illegal in most countries."

"Then what the hell are we waiting for?" He stood up so fast he almost knocked his chair over.

"I wanted to say goodbye to everyone." She sniffled. "Thank you all for making today the best day of my life. I love you. Every one of you."

"Crap. Not again." Morgan dabbed her eyes with the corner of a napkin. "Go on. Take your ridiculously handsome husband and get out of here."

"All right, then I guess there's only one more thing left to do." Kate bustled from her chair with Mike at her elbow for support. She made it halfway across the dance floor before peeking over her shoulder and taking aim.

She tossed her bouquet in Devon's direction.

It would have been a direct hit if not for the ceiling fan over their table.

A *whmmmp* similar to a table saw cut through the sappy music and the din of conversation before a shower of petals rained onto the rest of the crew. Devon raised her hands, palms up, to catch as much of the floral confetti as possible.

Rainbow colored bits of fauna decorated them all evenly.

The photographer Mike had hired swooped in close and took a candid picture of the disaster. Devon knew she would frame one of the standard portraits of the group they'd sat for earlier to hang in the living room of the apartment she shared with James and Neil.

But the snapshot he'd just captured would go in their bedroom.

It would live in the hearts and minds of the crew.

Forever.

WHAT HAPPENS TO THE CREW NEXT? KEEP READING TO FIND OUT!

NAILED TO THE WALL
POWERTOOLS
JAYNE RYLON
NEW YORK TIMES BESTSELLING AUTHOR

The crew is back and they're dirtier than ever.

Five sexy men with a penchant for love and lust in any variation have formed a crew. They work hard and play harder—together. Though their partnership began in construction, renovating houses and selling them for a mint, they've formed a bond around their shared goal to provide women, and each other, with the ultimate sexual experience.

Over the past year, as each member discovered his soul mate—or two—they expanded the reach of their circle, lighting up their nights along with their souls. Monogamous relationships and the desire to start families threaten to put their libertine revelry on the back burner. Will the passion that bonded them fade away? How will the new crew wives cope with the complex relationship the men will always cherish and crave?

Determined to prove they stand by their men, the women decide it's time to flex some muscle and give the crew a dose of girl power. They collude to take the guys as their horny hostages, using some big guns:

boudoir photos, a pillow fight and a calculated foray into partner swapping. But will they have the guts to go through with their plans?

Warning: By Book Five in this series, fans will attest that anything goes in the crew. Be prepared for ménage in every flavor—m/f, f/f, mfm, fmf, and more—along with a slew of that's what he said jokes. No throwing tomatoes at the author, please!

EXCERPT FROM NAILED TO THE WALL, POWERTOOLS BOOK 5

Devon popped another handful of caramel corn into her mouth, despite the fact that the credits of their third movie scrolled past on the muted TV. She smiled as she thought back to Dave and Kayla's first fight—a battle over the installment of the enormous flatscreen. Secretly, she was glad her friend had compromised and allowed the technology in her haven. The custom oak cabinet the crew had devised to hide any trace of ugly black plastic was a work of art.

Crispy, coated kernels surrendered to her chomping. She licked sticky sweetness from her fingers. When she looked up, she caught Kayla peeking at her from the corner of her eye.

Devon knocked her knee into her friend's. "Want some of this?"

"Yeah." Kayla made no move to grab a snack.

Morgan refilled their pretty, hand-blown margarita glasses. Colorful blobs encased in the clear material looked like confetti. They swirled and mixed in Devon's blurred vision. Last round for her. Being petite had been a curse she'd endured her entire life. Little to no tolerance for alcohol was a related inconvenience to suffer.

When Morgan finished serving them—all except Kate, who'd opted for fancy tea instead of booze—she plopped on the floor beside her best friend.

"So…" Kate leered at each of them in turn. "Truth or dare time."

"My favorite." Devon grinned.

"Good, then you first."

"Truth." She had no qualms about sharing herself with these women regardless of the silly game they played.

"Make it something juicy." Morgan poked Kate in the ribs. "You're evil at this. I should know. Remember when you forced me to admit my crush on your boyfriend in high school? Holy crap. I forgot his name. How can that be?"

"I think it was Tim. Or Ted maybe. Damn." Kate squinted. "It seemed like the end of the world at the time. Now that we have the crew, I can't help but think you saved me from potential disaster."

"Plus you got even in college with..." Morgan paused.

"Dan?"

"Uh, something like that. No, no, Doug. Definitely Doug." Morgan laughed. "I guess we've always had similar taste in guys."

"Great hormones think alike." Kate winked. "And now I know you've got it good with Joe."

"Lucky bitch." A slap on Kate's bared thigh accompanied the half-hearted curse.

"That's me. Anyhoo... It's been a while." Kate tapped her chin, then glanced at Kayla and Morgan. "I'm rusty. Help me. Both of you."

"Hell-oooo. You're the only sober one here." Kayla rolled her eyes. "You've got a pretty big advantage."

"Good point." Kate utilized their fit of giggles to consider. "Okay. But maybe we should change the rules. No singling anyone out. We'll all answer the question."

"Why the hell not?" Morgan shrugged. "We don't really believe in the whole solo thing around these parts. We're like the nine musketeers. Or is that three, three musketeers?"

"I can't do math after four margaritas!" Kayla rubbed her temples.

"You've had five," Kate corrected.

"You sort of proved her point." Devon nodded gingerly enough to avoid rattling her brains.

"Okay, okay." Kate held her hands up in surrender. "How about this? What's one thing you always hoped to try with our guys but haven't had the balls to go for yet?"

"Time to start planning our coup, huh?" Morgan clinked her glass against Kate's teacup.

"Yeah. I'll kick us off with some honesty of my own. Part of me is nervous. It's been a while now, coming up on two years, since I met the crew. I feel like we need to keep things fresh for Mike and the rest of them. They're used to adventure. I couldn't stand it if we didn't satisfy them as much as they've done for us." The rush with which the confession burst from Kate had them all sobering a tiny bit.

"You've thought about this a lot. Worried." Devon leaned forward to pat Kate's shoulder. "Mike adores you. You're all he really needs. You know that, right?"

"Yes." Kate swallowed hard enough for Devon to spot her throat flex. "I do. Deep down. That doesn't mean I don't want to give him the world. Better than only what he requires. Bare minimum isn't enough for the man of my dreams. We've also…"

"What, Katiebug?" Kayla defaulted to the nickname the guys had given their friend.

She released a dreamy sigh, then confessed, "Mike and I have toyed with starting a family."

"No wonder you're not drinking tonight." Kayla stared at the cup of tea clutched in Kate's white-knuckled grip.

"I've been dying to tell you all. I just…" She shook her head.

"You've been keeping too much inside." Morgan glared at Kate. "Don't you know we're here for you when you need us?"

"If we'd hidden something like this, you would have kicked our asses." Kayla leaned in closer. Morgan didn't harp, though. She glanced away, and her cheeks seemed to blush. Before Devon could dig deeper, Kate sighed.

"I know." At least she didn't attempt to deny it. "I'm sorry."

"So what's your main concern?" Devon tilted her head as she tried to decipher the issue.

"Once we have more responsibility, what if Mike is restless? As much as I can already feel a burning love for the baby we're praying for, I also know things will get harder. More stress. More obligation. More work. Our relationship could suffer. I'm terrified this brilliant magic we've created could fade into a perfectly comfortable, ordinary life. While he might be content, I can't imagine him happiest like that."

"Never forget we're a team." Morgan smirked. "With this many aunts and uncles to love a child, he or she won't be hard up for attention. And you'll never have to worry about a babysitter if you two need some time alone. Then, maybe someday, you could return the favor for Joe and me. Just think, our kids will grow up like brothers and sisters."

"That is nice to dream about." Kate brushed discreetly at the corner of her eye with a knuckle. "So I guess I'm going to answer my own stupid question. Tell me if I'm crazy."

"You are," Devon answered immediately.

"Brat." Kate's insult held no heat. Some of her seriousness dissolved. She took a deep breath, then admitted in a rush, "I'd like to watch one of you with Mike. I can't promise I won't get psycho jealous and try to rip you apart—gouge out your eyes or pull your hair or scratch you to shreds—but I'll do my best. I think he should have the option. And secretly, though he's never said anything, I think he's a touch jealous of the other guys. They got to be with some of you and he never did. Not that he wants to screw around or anything. But he's possessive. He considers all eight of us his in some way, you know?"

"You're both similar in that regard. Always taking care of the gang." Kayla grinned. "So how about a trade? Dave told me you were pretty damn hot that first time they shared you in the pool. I'm sure he'd be up for another taste. And he's plenty strong enough to keep your cat-fighting ninja moves in check should you make a break for me."

Devon noticed Morgan nodding in agreement. She thought about her relationship with the rest of the crew and how easy it would be to take the last step toward full-on intimacy. She loved each of the men for things they had in common as well as their individual strengths and quirks.

Morgan added softly, "I've grown so close to you all, and our guys. Most of us have been with some combination of them already…when we were first finding each other. One thing I've wondered about is making our sessions a free-for-all. The guys share each other. So why not us too? There are times, when we're all together, it would be so easy to reach out and touch Mike, Dave, Neil or James. They're gorgeous, and I love each of them. I'm sure I could improve their experience, same for them with me, but I'm afraid they're off limits. Why do we do that?"

Devon gnawed her lip. It was no secret Neil and James had played around with

every one of her friends before she entered
the picture. Truth be told, she imagined
sometimes what it would have been like to
be Kate. To have had all five men focused on
her pleasure.

Greedy much? Hell, yeah.

ABOUT THE AUTHOR

Jayne Rylon is a *New York Times* and *USA Today* bestselling author. She received the 2011 RomanticTimes Reviewers' Choice Award for Best Indie Erotic Romance.

Her stories used to begin as daydreams in seemingly endless business meetings, but now she is a full-time author, who employs the skills she learned from her straight-laced corporate existence in the business of writing. She lives in Ohio with two cats and her husband, the infamous Mr. Rylon.

When she can escape her purple office, Jayne loves to travel the world, SCUBA dive, take pictures, avoid speeding tickets in her beloved Sky and—of course—read.